# PEOPLE

# WHO

# DISAPPEAR

ALEX LESLIE

# PEOPLE
# WHO
# DISAPPEAR

*stories*

 FREEHAND BOOKS

Canada Council   Conseil des Arts
for the Arts     du Canada

Freehand Books gratefully acknowledges the support of the Canada Council for the Arts for its publishing program. ¶ Freehand Books, an imprint of Broadview Press Inc., acknowledges the financial support for its publishing program provided by the Government of Canada through the Canada Book Fund.

Freehand Books
515–815 1st Street SW Calgary, Alberta T2P 1N3
www.freehand-books.com

Book orders: LitDistCo
100 Armstrong Avenue Georgetown, Ontario L7G 5S4
Telephone: 1-800-591-6250 Fax: 1-800-591-6251
orders@litdistco.ca
www.litdistco.ca

**LIBRARY AND ARCHIVES CANADA CATALOGUING IN PUBLICATION**

Leslie, Alex
People who disappear / Alex Leslie.

Short stories.
ISBN 978-1-55481-059-8

I. Title.

PS8623.E845P46 2012      C813'.6      C2012-900306-9

Edited by Robyn Read
Book design by Natalie Olsen, www.kisscutdesign.com
Author photo by Lorraine Weir

Printed on FSC recycled paper and bound in Canada

# CONTENTS

# THE COAST IS A ROAD

1

**I KNOW THAT** travelling with you will be dangerous when all the wires blow down across the road on the way to Point No Point. Our first weekend away together. The wires, unravelled by the windstorm, hang from the poles. When you slow the car, I feel the pulse of dying electricity moving in the dark forest. You keep driving and I moan, staring through the window, you muttering, "That is not helping." My breath forms a solid column in the core of my body as we approach the first wire lying across the road. We cross. The texture of the road under the car's wheels plays my leg muscles like zithers. The second wire, the third. Each makes me breathe harder. The next will bring down my body, illuminate the forest like a magic lantern, show the bark down to the skin-like grain, the marks made by hungry searching birds. We've been sleeping together for a month, but this is when I start to trust your body, when we cross the last dead wire. The rest of the drive goes by in silence. We look through the windows and see what has been left behind by the storm. Rubble of huge cracked-open trunks, pulp of moss and ferns and leaves and needles mortared together by air made solid by speed, fresh trenches in the forest floor, wet black lines in the earth as if wires or veins had been torn up from underneath. The cabin, when we reach it, is quiet and cold. Ocean stretches calm from the edges of the windows.

For the next few days, we pass road crews clearing the mess away, sawing through trees that fell after we passed through. I try not to stare at the men scaling the electrical poles, standing in baskets like the crowsnests on ships, their orange-gloved hands working the wires. Was the current cut off completely before we drove through or did it continue, jagged and trying, moving like pain through an injured limb? I look down at your hand as it covers mine. Any of my friends would chalk to it up to shock, but I feel that the wires allowed us to cross over. It's a secret between us, a current between our bodies. In the winter daylight, the menace is gone, the wires high and taut in the still air, telegraphing nothing.

**2**

In the beginning, all we do is drive. The riddled coast is our hunting ground for concealed beaches, cheap motels, and restaurants serving only sandwiches, fried eggs, and beer-battered fish. I wait in motel parking lots while you go in to book the room, because these are tiny towns and we are two women. The rooms are all the same. Beds high and narrow as gurneys, calendar art, plumbing that gurgles and sucks like drainpipes during a rainstorm. These are our first rooms — not the small, separate spaces of our apartments, but these stripped-down cells in grey and paisley, live only with the sounds of us and footsteps of strangers on the ceilings and in the halls.

You go on these drives around the province for your reporting assignments — articles about the failing fisheries, protests against logging companies. "The usual," you say, and briefly I am thrown by how you see all of this as a taxonomy. Then I find this reassuring, your shrewd bird's-eye view of the world. The hours I spend watching your profile. Every few kilometres, your eye sweeps me sideways.

On the mornings I wake up in your studio apartment, I watch from bed as you fill mugs with your Bodum, pour in full cream from the half pint you keep only for coffee. This is one of the first things I notice — the attention you pay to small intense things. Cream for your coffee, the ten-dollar half-empty spice bottles crowding the second shelf of your cupboard, the semi-gloss paint you've used in your apartment, a different colour for every wall, directions standing out like disjointed panels of a circus tent.

You don't like to give direct invitations. My phone rings and I answer it to hear your voice saying, "Oil spill in Howe Sound, wind's pushing it north," or, "Whales migrating in the Broken Group Islands."

Trees flicker by like a film reel in grey and green, and the highway sweeps under the wheels until it is a faint line of colour like no other colour, a faint vein on the underside of the sky's skin, and we drive farther and farther away.

**3**

I've worked out of my apartment since quitting my last job at a documentary festival — indifferent grant writing that I tell myself is transitional, though it has become lazily long-term — and it's been easy to enter your mad routine of travel. You spend half the week roaming this part of the coast like an indigenous seabird, the other half locked in your studio apartment and following a migration route of coffee shops with your laptop, typing out articles.

It rains through the first three days we spend driving the road between Tofino and Ucluelet, drinking coffee thick as paint in cafés warm as nests, walking in and out of shops to finger sea-glass necklaces and dry our hair, wondering where all the people went and when we'll see some whales, as if they will swim onto the sidewalk in front of us out of the dark blue air. On the fourth day, the rain becomes snow and we set off down the highway toward home.

Evening and the thickening snow makes the world a dark glowing white where our headlights touch road and teeming grey where they touch air. The snowy road balanced against the side of the dark mountain, the ultrasound image of a bone inside an arm.

I say we should stop but you're the one driving.

"Why stop?" you say after a few minutes of silence. "It's getting worse and if we stop we'll be in the worse part, right?"

"Snow falls in the same thickness everywhere," I say. "It doesn't matter where we stop."

"This is not the time for Zen koans," you say.

You drive slowly—our wheels flattening crisp snow—and I jump out every few minutes to clear off the wipers. Snow has suddenly made the world featureless, intimidating as a burned face incapable of forming expression.

"Stop, I think we should stop," I repeat until you agree.

You can't pull over because the road's edges aren't distinguishable from the creeks, mountainsides, drop-offs — there are only the suggestions of curves that could be snow-shadows and moonlight. Where are the edges?

Snow swallows the darkness whole and you finally pull over. We crawl into the back seat, the snow encasing the car, the thickening cocoon drugging us. We fuck, our deep heat mixing with the cold, and I know that you could break my heart open like the wind.

"I got it used anyway," you whisper, your body balanced above mine.

"What?"

"The car."

"Oh."

"What did you think I meant?" you say and laughter makes your body hard to hold, a bundle of rope I'm trying to gather and keep in my arms. You always laugh at my misunderstandings like a child, mercilessly, then rub my shoulders to coax me back. "Oh sa-a-ad lady," you say.

A heavy wind starts up and plays the car like a tin drum. When you fall asleep, an hour before I do, your arms straighten and go limp. You roll away from me against the back of the seat. The air from your mouth comes out in cold white clouds and I press my palms against your cheeks to warm your skin.

The face in our window the next morning is a woman's, a road crew worker made cartoonish by the orange vest pulled over her Gore-Tex jacket. Her silver-and-black badge screams Emergency. Her face reddened more by cold or embarassment? The clothes and jackets we heaped sleepily on top of our bodies last night hide almost everything. There's nothing to do but wave, weakly, a hand to the cold glass. Her footsteps crunch in the icy crust along the side of the car and up the road.

In the road crew's truck, we drink coffee from their thermoses and listen to their stories about the snowstorm. Worst in near thirty years. Four big slides between here and Ucluelet. Old road so. Hell of a place for a storm, a peninsula, people getting trapped in like guys in a mine. We were damn lucky we kept driving. A man and his son got caught under a slide ten K back and the boy didn't pull through.

A sick tilt in my stomach. Dying in a snowslide would be worse than drowning, I think. No possibility even for a small struggle. Suffocation and cold combined for a mute finish. Were we making love when the boy died? Or had we still been driving? I push these questions away.

You are asking the appropriate things—do they have food for us, can we ride out in their truck, can they jumpstart our car? The battery drained from keeping up heat all night.

One of the men from the road crew offers to help, says, "Always happy to lend a hand to a damsel in distress." I watch you enjoy playing along, getting all your lines exactly right.

"Thank you," you repeat and he nods and nods. "*Thank* you." He can't get the car started. "Are the pipes frozen? Like in a house?" you say. He laughs and shakes his head, which makes him try harder, longer. I catch your elbow and you shake it off. If he catches on, I know, he'll turn on us with anger equal to his chivalry.

"Don't," I hiss in your ear. You shake me off again, grinning.

The worker who saw us through the car window, bodies tangled under yesterday's clothing, speaks into her handheld radio in the cut-out shadow of her truck, eyes narrowed against the cold.


The crew calls our motel hours later to say that your car still won't start. They pushed it to the side of the road for it to be towed out.

I lie on the bed, my body aching, cold with the feeling of danger that didn't play itself out. Your body bright against the window. Your body last night in the car, all the snowlight reflecting through the window, the lit ice of your skin. You look down at the parking lot, frowning. Before lying down beside me, you take the Gideon bible off the bedside table and toss it into the mini fridge.

"What're you thinking about? Lying here glowering," you say, your arms spread out around you. One of your teeth yellow because half the time you're too lazy to brush, the tooth like an unusual stone you keep hidden in your mouth. When you first started staying over at my apartment, I bought a toothbrush for you at London Drugs, knowing you would never bring your own. I already knew the obvious details you couldn't see, the routines obvious to other people that you glided around. It made me want to fill in all the invisible things for you. When I gave you the toothbrush, you thanked me and hugged me, placed it in the cup beside my sink, and never used it once.

"It isn't such a disaster," you're saying. You wedge a hand between my back and the quilt. "They're towing the car back. I have insurance." You stretch your other arm across my stomach.

"It isn't funny," I say, turning toward the wall.

You kick gently at my ankles, the length of your body edging closer, warmer.

"What isn't funny?" you say.

"Doom," I say.

You begin to laugh. After a few seconds, I join in. Guiltily at first, then with loose gasps that lurch harsh and relieved from my stomach. Your laughter comes out in tall, sharp waves like reckless shouts.

"Maybe we should stop doing this so much," I say.

"Doing what?"

"Driving."

"It's what we do best," you say.

I don't even own a car. Too expensive, I've always thought. When I first told you that, you snapped back, "You can only know this part of the coast if you own a car."

You tighten a hand around my shoulder and I weaken, roll over. The hotel room has grown uncomfortably hot.

"You want to give up that easily?" you say.

**4**

A day's frantic travel to get from your apartment in downtown Vancouver to Desolation Sound, the last stop on the highway up the Sunshine Coast. It always stuns me that remote twists of mist and rock are within a day's drive of the city's packed-in smoke. You honk your car horn over and over in the new morning dimness, and I see your headlights over the edge of my windowsill as I pull on my shoes, stumble for the door. Two short ferry trips. Hours of road. Chasing the smooth line of highway into the dark v of trees, giant Douglas firs arrowing the sky's highway neck. The town here, Lund, was originally a trading post between settlers and Aboriginal people, you say as the road turns, slopes sharply into the dark elbow of water, the old hotel dominating. You're here to interview marine biologists about the ocean reserve. Toxicity in the water is on the rise. Whole forests are being poisoned from beneath the surface, you tell me. The back seat is covered with your research. Your laptop slides back and forth across the overlapping papers like a smooth flat stone. While you do your interviews I walk in and out of tiny shops, browse the coastal kitsch. Candles studded with small shells; framed photographs of amber Western light weakening in folds of sand, stone, a heron out there on the horizon, one leg like a pylon holding the sky and ocean apart; lumpy mugs stencilled with starfish; sea-glass pendants swinging from black silk cords. I sit on a bench overlooking the harbour. A half-sunken houseboat out there, its roof sticking up above the surface of Desolation Sound like a cocked hat. The air beginning to darken, the slackening ocean casting silver stripes at the blind regions among the clouds. I watch a small boy hurl hunks of bread at a seagull and wonder how I got here, to this remote end of highway, how I lost the need to will my own life. A tin can rattling, small tin rabbit jumping, tied to your bumper. You find me sitting on the bench after dark, waiting for you. You smell like the people you've been interviewing, faint brine of strangers. Another hotel room. Your body on the sheet like paint thrown against a wall that has dripped accidentally into the shape of a woman.

**5**

What is it I feel near you? The sight of wires slicing the road, the stunned nerves in the backs of my hands as we crossed over. When we take the ferry to Vancouver Island, I go out onto the deck, regardless of the weather. Active Pass slips its dark form around me. Glass houses levitating from the rock are lanterns on night sailings, marking the route for the ferry. The occasional eye-blink of a lighthouse. Air thrown up by the ocean rushes down the deck and makes my stomach its windsock. Ocean noise — underground weather.

There's a direct ferry to Saltspring Island from Tsawassen, the terminal near Vancouver, but I misread the BC Ferries schedule in your glove compartment and we end up on the ferry that stops at every gulf island.

"The fucking whistle-stop ferry," you say, your body turned like a hook in one of the seats behind the huge window at the prow. Bag of White Spot from the ferry cafeteria steaming in your lap. The sailing is three and a half hours instead of one and a half. Gabriola. Galiano. Pender. Saturna. At every island, the ferry pushes slowly into the tiny berth, opens its maw, and spills the islanders out, the first row of car hoods like shining teeth.

"Sorry," I repeat, and you stare wordlessly into your reflection in the window. "Are you going to stop taking me with you?" — as soon as the words come out, I feel my face heat up. I see your smile shimmering on the dark glass. "It's not funny," I say.

"What's not funny?" you say.

I open my bag of food. You refused to eat in the ferry cafeteria, said only, "The sound of screaming children ruins even the best real estate," turned and walked away, leaving me to order the food and find you afterward in the best seats at the prow, watching the ocean.

I feel you watching me as I tear off chunks of chicken fingers, chew the battered greasy meat, add french fries, and drink Pepsi from my sweating cup. "Nothing," I say.

"You eat like a little kid," you say.

"Why can't you leave me alone."

"Oh sa-a-ad lady," you coax, rubbing my shoulders. When I give in and lean toward you, you stretch an arm around me and mutter, "It doesn't matter about the direct sailing. This is a great way to get in some people-watching."

A toddler hurtles by in a Spiderman costume. An adult's beckoning yell from the back row, like a heckler in a movie theatre, the sound forceful and pointless. The tiny superhero tries a pirouette, enjoying the red-and-blue smudge of himself in the window. Outside, seagulls play in the air pocket made by the ferry. Fling upward, plummet.

"I'm never having guppies," you say, watching the toddler fall and fall. A few silent minutes pass before you add, "Amanda wants to have more guppies." The word "more" just a garrotted bark. Amanda's your older sister. Straight, married to a lawyer, a businesswoman with two degrees in engineering — something to do with geothermal technology — and three boys. These were the coordinates you offered after we ran into her at a movie. You introduced me as your travelling companion and Amanda smiled at me with watchful curiosity. She wore copper jewellery and carried a Puma shoulder bag. You're the middle child. A younger brother teaches overseas.

"What does Amanda think of us?" I say.

You shrug. "She said you seemed great."

"Do you get along?"

"Most of the time. We don't talk that often. I'm probably kind of a satellite sibling to her helicopter parent," you say and laugh loudly at your own joke.

"Satellite," I say, the word pressing into me like a new bruise.

"Amanda described me once as picking up my bag and getting lost on the coast," you said. "I liked that."

I feel something inside me tear slowly away from itself. You are nothing I can keep.

A ferry worker comes around and begins pulling the black covers over the windows.

"When I was a kid," you say, "I thought they put those covers up to hide horrible storms happening outside. I thought that all the way through till I was a teenager. Then my dad told me it's for navigation, so all the light from inside doesn't go out, fool other boats."

You've mentioned having relatives on the north part of Vancouver Island — called simply "The Island" by natives of this part of the coast.

"You went over to the island a lot when you were a kid?" I say.

"My dad worked over there a lot, so sometimes I'd just go for the ride."

"Where'd he work?"

"Prisons. Planned them. So he travelled around a lot. For the government."

"Really? Did you go inside?"

Over the months we've travelled together — over eight months, I count quietly in my mind — this is the most you've told me about your childhood. I know that your mother died when you were a toddler and that your father has never re-married. Once when I asked what you were like as a kid, you answered, frowning, "I think I was born as a little old man."

"No, he never took me inside," you say. "I just liked going for the trip. I liked the ferry. I stayed in the car in the parking lot. This one prison, near Nanaimo, was my favourite because I'd sit and pick blackberries through the window and eat them until he came back."

"Did you ever see any of the prisoners?"

"Only once."

"Once?"

"I'll tell you some other time."

The seats have gone quiet, the superhero asleep on the carpet in a corner. You pull a folded map of Saltspring out of your pocket and point to the part of the island where we'll be staying. You trace a nearby faint blue line with your finger. "You see that road? Scared the hell out of me once. The end of it just goes right out onto these shelves of rock. You're not careful you could drive right into the ocean."

**6**

Your editor gives you an assignment that requires travelling to the northern part of the province. You'll be travelling for all of May and June.

You tell me this sitting at the scratched-up walnut table pushed up under the large window in your apartment. You found the table on the side of the road in West Vancouver, on a sloped street of cedar and glass houses shone through with the Pacific. You got the table into the back of your car, tilting and pivoting it on one leg after the other, alternating directions until you could flip it and slide it in. What had you done for a table before? I wanted to know — I was picturing you wrestling the heavy table around the road, the neighbours carefully navigating around you in their hushed Porsches. "I don't know," you said. "I never really needed a table before. I never thought about it." It frightened me, in the beginning, how much you didn't notice, didn't know was necessary.

You've always wanted to go on the ferry up the Inside Passage, you say — the route that begins near Port Hardy at the northern end of Vancouver Island, passes among the islands and inlets of the coast, an eighteen hour sailing north that docks in Prince Rupert. Then the seven hour ferry across Hecate Strait to the Queen Charlotte Islands.

You're unfolding a map that covers the table. A large compass kilometres in diameter floats out in the middle of the ocean. "This whole part of the coast I don't know at all," you say, smoothing the map gently with your palm. Two side-by-side islands like twisted crabs: Dolphin Island, Spicer Island. Fine lines etch the depths of the ocean. A much larger island, shaped like a fetus: Porcher Island.

Your voice, as you say these names, sways toward tenderness. I recognize this voice from your articles that I look for every day in the newspaper. I know that sometimes you don't take me with you on trips. You confessed to me last month that you've been offered the job of section editor several times. But you need to keep moving, need the long pulls of stories, the possibility of a landscape of immediate things.

"You gotta be somewhere?" you say, watching me get up from my chair.

"Yeah, work."

"You work from home," you say.

For a moment I'm surprised that you know this about me. How much do you know about my days? For months I've skipped most messages from my friends. A friend, Jessica, who I've been close to since undergrad, left a message last week saying only, in a distant, clipped voice: "Um, call me sometime." When the message played, I was getting ready to leave to meet you for a late-night coffee; I forgot to call her back.

"I have to go," I say, struggling with the strap of my bag that has suddenly come alive and twists out from under the grip of my fingers again and again. "I don't know what we're doing with this. I don't know what we're doing."

You stand and watch me quietly.

"I was going to ask you to come," you say.

For once you don't make fun of me. This is how you give hugs: you put your arms out on either side and I lean into you as if are a tree.


Travellers stand in the rain talking about the ferry going up the coast. The ferry will be three days late, the tired women in the office just told all of us. BC Ferries will pay for the necessary nights of accommodation. We're trapped here, in this outpost on the northern end of Vancouver Island, until then.

"It's the way with BC Ferries, since they went corporate," says a man from Comox, his wife in matching cherry-red Gore-Tex nodding hard.

A German man whose plan was to catch a second boat to Alaska in Prince Rupert and then fly home to Frankfurt from Whitehorse stands on the dark pavement, looking lost. "What will I do now?" he says.

You shrug. "It's the way things go on this part of the coast, you know?" you say — something you've said to me too many times to count. The German regards you, eyebrows falling over his hard eyes. I see you for a moment through his devastating point of view. A small, compact woman with an ease of speech too easily mistaken for arrogance.

"That is unhelpful," he says. His English is poor and formal. "I am right to have trust in the schedules."

"Why don't you just drive back to Victoria and get on a plane, then?" you say. You have no respect for rigid people, I know, and as we drive away to search for a motel not overrun by truckers or tree planters, you mimic the shrill exchange we've just left. The human exchange of news that you hear as poetry for dummies, an inane recitation among strangers, a children's book chant.

*The ferry is late.*

*The ferry is still very late.*

*Did you see the black bear on the road?*

*It was a big black bear?*

*Yes!*

*How big?*

*Really big.*

*Which road was the big black bear on?*

*On the road.*

*On which road?*

*Which road?*

*On the road to town.*

*Where was the big black bear on the road?*

*On the middle of the road.*

*The big black bear was on the middle of the road on the way to town?*

*Yes!*

*The ferry is late.*

*The ferry is still very late.*

We drive through the scrappy north island towns — Chevron, Overwaitea, one government-issue high gloss totem pole for every RCMP station. The Cold Beer and Wine Store attached to the Family Restaurant attached to the eighteen-wheeler's motel of choice. We don't need to tell each other that the motels where men sit outside their rented room doors in dirty work pants eating burgers out of paper bags, bottles of liquor tipsy on the pockmarked concrete beside their boots, would not be safe for us.

Finally, you pull up to a hotel painted in white and forest green, a statue of a black bear standing upright on either side of the office door. "Looks white bread enough," you say. "This must be where the BC Hydro guys stay."

Another hotel room. How many hotel rooms have I shared with you? These plain, anonymous spaces that float free of home and routine. Two months of this, driving together.

You set up your laptop on the table while I cook rice from the large bag in the trunk of your car and chicken thighs we picked up in Overwaitea. When we travelled together before, the trips never more than two or three days long, we got by on cheap restaurant food and gas station sandwiches. This is the first time we've shopped together, selected food, planned meals beforehand. The hard rhythm of your typing and the spitting of the chicken skin crisping in the pan. The low hum of your writing fills the room.

The ferry waits in the dark morning light, sleeps in the water in the rocky cove like a huge white whale. We stand on the deck and watch the island leave us, drift free and move northward.

The coast slides past the windows, dawn to night, dark to next dark, all the way north. Whale backs sink dark ink into polished water. The setting sun sears the water gold two hours before we meet earth in Prince Rupert, bump off the ramp into darkness.

Then across Hecate Strait. The night ferry. Seven hours across the night's flat open back. We climb the narrow metal stairs from the vehicle deck, unroll our sleeping bags between two rows of seats, then sit leaning against each other to watch the mainland slip away. Islanders returning home from the mainland congregate around the doors. Most Haida, some white. Women pull out decks of cards and start games of gin rummy. A young father coaxes his daughter into her pyjamas, asks her to pick a story to read before sleep. They crawl together to sit in the Coke machine's gentle lantern glow and she opens the book slowly. Passengers settle down for sleep among the seats. The quiet slip-slip of the group of women dealing and throwing down cards, occasional soft groans of dreaming, the low machine thoughts of the ferry making its way out to open water. The tall orange lights of the port sail past like dark stars. Three silvery teenage boys share a laptop screen in the far corner. From their strained faces, I knows it's porn they're watching. Their parents peacefully asleep at their toes.

"Ready for sleep?" you whisper.

I hear the teenage boys snickering behind their laptop across the tops of the seats when you slip out of your sleeping bag and unzip mine.

"What if someone wakes up?" I hiss back.

"Are you kidding? This thing is the boat of the living dead," you respond, moving your hands around my hips, and I wonder how many people have made love on this sailing, the quiet of the night water and sounds of sleeping humans spreading around, the calmly advancing ferry a small secure shuttle between worlds.


The Queen Charlotte Islands —"Haida Gwaii," you correct me — rise out of the Pacific in long sloping fingers of green and black. Their landscape untouched by the ice age, you tell me. An ancient geography. You love to point out the signs reading Tsunami Evacuation Route, laughing. "If there's a tsunami and we're in a car, we'd better hope it floats," you say. "That's the only evacuation route. Away from the bottom of the ocean."

"Don't be morbid," I say.

"It's not morbid, it's true. It's the only romantic myth about living on the coast worth believing. If there's an earthquake or a tsunami, we're all gone. Nothing left. Might as well see it that way. Look it in the eye."

"Nobody can live that way," I say, and you don't answer.


The next day, flipping through the guest sign-out book in the small cabin we're renting, you let out a yell, then pull the book off the table, laughing. "Look, look."

I read the entry beside your finger, written to cabin's owners:

*Dear Jackson and Lorna,*
*Thank you for your wonderful hospitality and warm welcome. We really appreciated your help when the ocean took our car at North Beach.*
*Sincerely,*
*Ellen and Cam O'Brien*

It's a common thing that happens to tourists, we learn the next morning from the woman, Krystal, who sells us our morning coffees and fried egg and bacon sandwiches in the gas station twenty minutes from our cabin. Men in working clothes sit on stools around the counter, their plates crowding up against the cash register and jars of chocolate mint patties and beef jerky. Krystal presides, her body like a wedding cake on toothpicks. Two brown front teeth, a seductive sea lion smile.

"People drive their cars right out onto the sand on North Beach, you know, thinking it's all fun and all. Then they leave their cars for a bit and go for a walk up the beach. Well it's a real long beach, you know. Long walk, hour and more, out to Rose Spit, and that's where they all want to go, all the tourists, so they can stand out there and feel all at the edge of the world with water all around them. Like it's their romantic moment, like that part in the Titanic movie or whatever. And they come back and their car's gone. First they think some teenager's stolen it. But then they see there aren't no wheel marks. And then they start thinking. It's the ocean. It comes up any time and takes what it wants." She breaks down into lungburst laughter and fills our coffees back up for free.

Two men at the end of the counter count their crippled fingers, exchange news about workers' compensation. "Got money for this one, not for this one, got more for this one."

"I could interview them," you tell me under your breath. "They probably used to work on the fishing boats. When there were still fish." I've become accustomed to the alertness of your journalist eye. You can talk to any stranger, manoeuvre their sentences toward the information you want. When we first met I could tell when you were nervous with me by the shift in your voice toward an interview tone —"Stop interviewing me," I'd say savagely, the only way I could startle you into silence. "This isn't an interview. I am the person you're talking to."

You drive the road to North Beach — the northernmost end of Haida Gwaii — with crazed anticipation. A long dirt road through forest cloaked in moss, all angles erased by dark green light. This part of the island has been ceded to the Haida, you say, but it was probably logged before that. Hard to believe,

I think, staring into the world under the rainforest's canopy, curtains and hollows.

North Beach spreads away, flat and bright, vanishing off to the right into distance, curving beyond the eye's reach to Rose Spit, a sand peninsula fading off into the Pacific, pointing the way to Alaska. Turning around, I see the hill we've just passed, a dark rough thumb of volcanic rock. "This is where the Haida say everything started, you know," you say, walking quickly ahead of me across the sand. "This is where raven found humans in a clam shell." We walk for twenty minutes along the water and Rose Spit seems no closer, the white sand spreading sun-smoothed around us, distanceless. A family has parked their red truck up near the bank of logs washed in by the ocean. Their barbecue releases a fine column of smoke, backlit by the sun. "Hope they don't get swept out." At the end of Rose Spit, there is only ocean around us, a tiny scrap of sand we stand on above the water. The island's long mist ghost clings at our backs.

This is where you begin to tell me the story about the astronaut. You were eight years old, eating blackberries in a parking lot, waiting for your father. You're the only one who saw him.

When we walk back along the beach, the family and the red truck are gone. "Guess they got swept away," you say. I stare at the place where they were, the sun-bleached logs, the heaped leg bones of dinosaurs. I force myself to believe that something as heavy as a pick-up could be removed so simply, instantly. Slid off under the ocean's dark blue sweep like a pill under a tongue. Wouldn't humans on the beach hear the tide changing its thoughts, thundering in? Thousands of tons of water turning on a dime. Gravity's leg swinging inward. We walk toward the forest. I hear only the regular beat of the water on the sand, the nearing trees rubbing their large soft bodies against each other, wind-turned seabird wails.

You find the tire prints where they turned the pickup around. Their turning circle like a lopsided sundial in the sand, all the indentations full of shadow in strong contrast to the beach's smooth bright wash. I kneel and press my fingers into the prints, turn my head toward the ocean's endless span. The air at eye level fills with water and drains into a brightness that gives hard skin to every living thing.

### 7

On the crossing back to the mainland, the ferry pitches across Hecate Strait like a tin can in a gutter, and we both give up the warm waters of our insides.

The passenger seat takes on the shape of my body. The curves in the road take on the shape of our conversations. I watch your eyes in the rear-view mirror. You take calls from your editor and from William on your cell. Otherwise it's just us. You drive us across the top of the province, stopping in every small town.

We keep a running list of things. The dozens of eagles like sentries on the electrical poles and wires by the towers of crab traps in Prince Rupert. The latkes on the breakfast menu at the motel restaurant in Terrace.

I've sublet my apartment to a friend who's in grad school and was grateful for the space for a couple months at less than full rent to finish her thesis. When I think of returning to my apartment, filling it with the things I'll carry back from this trip, I'm stunned by the cold already swelling inside me. Mornings are something slack and light.

I dream that you're driving your car on the ocean floor, taking long lazy turns among the curious whales, jagged bases of reefs, your face lit up inside the car's glass-lantern shell, the purple sides mirrors for fish. I am somewhere in the water, watching you, my pickled eyes watching, jealous and terrified, as you drive through darker and darker layers of water until you're gone entirely.


You guard your notebook like a gate, but leave your papers lying loosely everywhere. I didn't know you kept a notebook before this trip.

In Prince George, the last city before we set off down the highway toward the lower mainland and Vancouver, the end of our trip, I wait for you to sleep, then take my arms away from your body and find your notebook under your sweaters in your bag.

I've been expecting bad or elliptical poetry; or journal entries full of your usual long cryptic descriptions of people and things; or transcriptions of the conversations you eavesdrop on in coffee shops and restaurants. What I find makes my hands grow warm in the darkness, kneeling on the floor on the thin carpet. Descriptions of all of our trips together; a list of junk food we've bought at gas stations; a list of ferry sailings we've taken and missed, waited for in dark parking lots, people walking their desperate dogs between the rows of cars; a list of the places I've gone with you, and a parallel list of the places you've gone alone. I shut the notebook without finishing and push it back to the bottom of your bag, return to find you still sleep-ing in the bed.

On the last day of the trip we hit gridlock all the way through the valley on the way into Vancouver. We sit in traffic, inching forward. The wild speed of the trip leaves our bodies. You leave the radio on through all of these hours. We don't talk. When you drop me off at the curb outside my apartment, you get out to help me with my bag, automatically heave yours onto the curb too. I help you throw it back in and watch you drive away.

**8**

After the trip north, sex changes. Your hands slip rapid fire around my body. You're searching for something, trying to find something in the deep pockets where you think I keep things hidden. I know the soft interlockings of your muscles and bones, know the chart of your body better than any ultrasound, my palms picking up the throbs and weakening pulses. Some nights you wrap your right leg around my left leg like a bandage and do not speak. "You should never leave me," you say. The words send a charge looping through my chest. An electric eel set loose inside me, touching every edge with its dark hot tongue.

Something about us has become more tangible to others, I can tell — we're now often asked how we met. I let you improvise, watching how you weave in parts of real stories, enjoying your inventions.

We were stranded on the same highway during a snowstorm, your battery had died, and you came to my car for heat. "Heat," you repeat hoarsely and your audience laughs. We met during a windstorm. Electrical wires had been blown down across the road and neither of us, in our separate cars, had wanted to drive over the possibly live wires, and that was how we met, sketched into a small space by the invisible, powerful current. We met on the night ferry somewhere in the middle of Hecate Strait. We had sex in the light from the Coke machine.

"So romantic," people say, some knowing enough to doubt you.

"Hard to believe but true," you say.


You've parked below on the street in front of my building and honked and honked and woken up the neighbours early in the morning too many times to count. This time you sit quietly in the front seat and light a rare cigarette. You only smoke when you're nervous. I watch you from my kitchen window, half expecting you to change your mind and drive away. I watch you smoke the cigarette down to its end, throw it out the window into a puddle, light another, and get out of your car, flip the car door shut behind you, head toward the front door to come upstairs and help me carry down the boxes full of all my things to drive to your apartment.


**9**

When you were eight years old, you sat in a car with your father and he drove to a gravel parking lot outside a prison on Vancouver

Island. You passed a sign that said CORRECTIONAL FACILITY above the name of the prison. You asked your father what language the name was in and he shrugged and said, "I think it's from a First Nations word or something." He stopped the car in the bank of dark shade at the far end of the parking lot under a tangled overhang of blackberry bushes and rolled your window half-way down, the three other windows all the way up. "I'll just be a few minutes," he said. "Want me to leave the radio on?" He knew you always wanted the radio on. You still do. You've told me that it's a force of habit from spending so much time driving — your need to have the sound of another voice in the car. "Before you," you add carefully. You have detailed judgments of the impulsive jokes and grasping segues of all the local DJs, as if they're people you've known long enough to criticize within earshot, cut mid-speech with one of your perfect interruptions.

It was hot in the car. Sunlight flared up along the edges of the shade. Your dad had left the radio on an AM station that played oldies. You knew the lyrics to every song for the first twenty minutes. You watched the clock. Knowing the words that sounded out of empty space made you feel masterful. You still know all the lyrics to those songs, haven't forgotten any of your childhood knowledge.

After a while, bored, you got up on your knees and stuck your head out the window. The wide eye of the windshield wasn't enough. You needed to see for yourself. Turned your neck around all the way, like you'd seen in *The Exorcist.* Looked at the sky.

The song playing was "Going to the Chapel." And we're gon-na get mar-ar-ar-ied. You sang the words loudly across the wide gravel lot. Go-ing to the chap-el of love!

The blackberry bush showed columns of dark fruit to you

when you grasped a branch and dragged it downward. Pebbles of flavour, a tight cluster like insect eyes. You relished this gross thought. The blackberries were warm when you picked them. You were surprised by their small, steady heat in the centre of your hand. You opened the door of the glove compartment and began loading the berries.

You stood on the seat and braced your belly on the edge of the window, looted branches deeper and higher. You don't remember the music that played during this part. Had it been half an hour since he'd left? More?

The glove compartment was half full and you already imagined giving the blackberries to the relatives up-island, saying something casual and impressive, "Thought these might come in handy for a dessert." You felt like a provider. Your thin body, hard and straight, before puberty when you put on the weight that made you shy away from strangers until you came out during undergrad. Your wrists scratched up with the delicate razors of thorns.

When the alarm blared from the prison, you thought for a second it was the radio. A short-circuiting of all the signals, a single overbearing voice from the world.

You let go of branches and fell downward.

One cheek rubbed hard against the gravel. Smashed purple fruit leaking from your fist, stained like a vein down your arm. You lay stunned at the bottom of the shade.

You heard your father yell your name.

Where are you where are you? He could not see you.

You turned your face, not knowing half of it was covered in blood, and saw with one eye the man in the orange suit standing deep in the blackberry bushes.

This is the only story you have never told anyone else, you tell me.

The man in orange was mostly hidden by the branches. Colour flared off him and he stepped back into the shadow. You smiled at him.

You thought he was an astronaut. The alarm was to tell everyone that his rocket had crashed.

You said hello to the man in the orange suit. He held up one hand, then held one finger against his lips. You nodded. He was a secret astronaut. You understood that. You wanted him to trust you. He stood there, looking at you, just standing there. You thought he seemed kind of awkward. Maybe just shy. A new planet would be hard.

Your cheek burned. You put your hand on it and it came off stamped red. It hurt less than all that blood made it look.

The alarm coming from the prison screamed and screamed. You noticed that his suit wasn't puffy at all, like an astronaut's should be. It hung limply from the frame of his body. He was thin, from all that time eating canned food and bread in outer space.

The man mouthed to you: Are you okay?

You mouthed back: I'll be fine.

Your father was yelling your name from somewhere. His voice was different than you had ever heard it. And you heard heavy shoes slamming on gravel. Men's feet running. You stood up and went around the front of the car.

The alarm stopped, the world fell into silence.

You wondered why your father seemed so scared.

He yelled, "What happened? Where were you?"

You said, "I fell out the window."

There were a bunch of men behind him in blue uniforms

with gold badges. Three of them held guns. They'd all come out of the prison, you guessed.

No one asks you if you've seen anything. Prisoners always ran in the opposite direction, away from the parking lot and the highway. Everyone runs into the forest.

It was years before you thought of that, though — it was years before any of the details began to present themselves to you. You were twelve or thirteen by then. The astronaut was faint and strong, a pulse of orange light in your memory, a message in the radio stream from the rest of the universe. Sometimes you told yourself that you'd invented him, to make yourself forget. Whenever your father went away for a few days to visit a prison, you said goodbye to him coldly, sending him into strangeness. For years after you saw the prisoner in the bushes, you thought of your father's trips as voyages to other planets. Slaves in orange suits walked these worlds.

Your father carried you into the prison to be cleaned up. He hadn't carried you in years and you were surprised by how easily he lifted you from the ground. In a brightly lit room where a few men lay on beds, a nurse had you sit on a table and she gently cleaned your cheek. In the hallway, you stopped at a small window and looked into a room full of tables where men in orange uniforms worked silently, and then your father pulled you away. In the car, he looked at the motherload of blackberries, your gleaming dark pile of treasure, closed the glove compartment hard. Said, "Okay to go?" You drove for hours down the highway that stretched along the spine of the island, wordless. After a while, dark juice began to leak out around the bottom edge of the glove compartment door, drip bright spots of warm colour onto your knees.

In that parking lot, you were changed. I know that and I know that's why you told me this story. I prod but you won't say what the story means to you. When I try to ask, you frown and repeat parts of it as your answer. "I don't know . . . The prisoner asked if I was okay," you say, or "I guess . . . I fell out of the window and I didn't think I would see anyone in the bushes," and you stop and look away, sorting events in your mind, or thinking nothing at all, only remembering.

**10**

We're drinking orange pekoe and sharing a plate of chicken fingers in the ferry cafeteria when we feel the boat start to go down. On the deck — darkness, BC Ferries staff calm-faced and loud-voiced as soldiers in their navy uniforms, the ocean keening under the bright lights. The ocean, suddenly all there, everywhere, a live thing waiting for us to enter it. Active Pass around us, Vancouver less than an hour away. One of your hands grasps one of my thighs. One of my hands finds one of your shoulders. Night becomes electric. Where is the water?

"Into the boats, folks, into the boats," voices recite in the darkness. The opening line of a psalm caught on repeat. For months I will wake at night beside you in the darkness, hearing voices ordering, "Into the boats, into the boats."

Already the throaty noise of helicopters caught somewhere above the clouds. Past the light shining down where it smashes on the water and is hurled back up. A man between us and one of the boats overflowing with kids in rubber and fleece, primary colours and open eyes and mouths, is asking a ferry worker about his car. The ferry worker says softly that the doors to the lower decks have been sealed and would you please get into the emergency craft with your family, sir. The man climbs over the white edge and falls onto the shoulders of his children.

My body is something separate and wild, a flag I have been handed to wave in the wind. Where are you? Coaxing, wrestling me into one of the boats. One hand for each side of my lower back, your fingers make hard braces for my muscles that run downward like water. As the boat goes down, I look up across the ferry's broad side. Pale spots — skin, faces, then the faces move across a width of darkness into the last boat. The ferry's side angles off, polished slickly by the moon, like a butcher knife stuck crooked into the sky. The boat's motor fast away from the dying mountain of it. The ferry begins to slip under, a great sound like tired-out thunder.

The dogs. We hear them barking, barking. Are the cars on the lower deck already surrounded by water? Your face slips between the searchlights slashing valleys in the water, bounces like a rubber ball, and I put my hands out to hold it still.

The dogs. Yells, silence, the whole ocean moving out there like a black planet, the tiny boat darting and sliding. You take chicken fingers out of your pocket and we bite into the soft greasy meat, hunching under the whiplash wind. You slide to the bottom of the boat and I squat between your chest and legs, lean slightly into you. This is the first time I've thought of you as something fragile, as anything but tightly-coiled and firm. Your arms a brittle hoop around me — if I move, I could snap your elbows. Your body a small house to crouch inside. I settle down, frozen.

I press the back of my head against your open mouth, feel the heat of your breath in my hair.

That something so large and unassuming, the commuter calm of a ferry, could fall, your body left sinking into cold water, holding onto other cooling bodies, colours escaping like fading siren sound.

Screams.

"People are still on there?" I hiss, not wanting the children to hear me. But everybody on the ocean can hear the screams.

"No. Horses," a man's voice says from the other side of the boat. He's travelling alone. I notice his black leather pants that shine like the water. "Trailers of horses with the trucks. Heading over to a race on the mainland."

A horse's kicking legs would be uncontrollable underwater. Great slashing things, lashing free all the junk of the world.

Our chests buckle together. Freezing spray comes over the edge of the boat. You lean forward and your heat is all around me. The screams of the drowning horses speed out across the churning water as the ferry goes under, screams sharp and reeling as the sirens of the rescue boats when they come.

# SPILL

**TO SEE HER**, you take the boat from the city to the island. She lives on the island, on the same street, a street of buildings full of people she does not talk to. She talks to you, when you come.

Between, there is water.

In the water, there is oil. The oil is all over the news, a smear of glistening belly, words swirled onto the skins of beasts strangled by the slickness. Ducks and whales and seals. Bundles of wet black. Otters, herons, sea lions. All the faces look the same.

–What did they expect, she says. What did they expect when you can see six freighters any time day or night. There'd be a big spill sooner or later. And they act so surprised.

–I read in the paper, you say, that they were sold a defective tanker.

–You believe that? All they care about is that oil they lost.

She puts a picture from the newspaper on her fridge. The first beached whale. The fine blanket of shimmer tethered to its dorsal.

Another picture on the fridge. The coast on fire. The sunset. Slim line of lit gas.

–The sunset, she says. Look at that. They made it even better.


You take the boat to the island where she lives, where she is always waiting with the news about the way things really are. She knows. She spends her time watching the news, and, when the news isn't on, watching documentaries she gets from the library, until she can't walk that far. Six whole blocks. And the state of her feet.

–It's all going to Hell, she says. You're so unlucky, to be young. I can't imagine what it will be like when you're as old as I am. I'm glad I'm not going to hang around long enough to watch it all go downhill.

The oil clean-up. Animal rescue volunteers squirting electric-blue Dawn dish soap onto wings. Ducks slip around in the cupped white human hands, as if they've just been born.

–Dawn dish soap works on oil, she says. I read about it in last Tuesday's paper.

The oil touching everything. A panoramic shot of the coast from Portland to Alaska — the black etch and drift of the spill.

–Oil cleanup, she laughs. Like putting toothpaste back in the tube. That's what they said about saying evil words when I was little.

She puts a picture of the oil tycoons on the fridge, beside the picture of the whale. Polished skin to match their suits. The men stand in a row, their heads bowed as if in prayer. Heavy watches shackle their white wrists. The photographer's strategic angle has placed a protestor's placard above their shoulders: WHY? SPILL!

–The faces, she says. Always pay attention to people's faces.


The boat you take to the island passes close to where they've contained the oil. For a while, the government stopped the boats. Then they started again.

Inflated orange snakes bob on the surface. To contain poison, or flame? You wonder which.

You look hard at the water. Can you see it there? Or is that light, is that the colour of motion? The blue eye of escaping oil. Soft-edged electric ridges. Or the tide, or the backs of fish?

The boat, government-regulation white, rinsed again and again. The tide dutifully circulates.

You stand on the deck. The wind rips your head off.

You hurt, a million sharp fins slapping.

You watch the sunset, how it bleeds and lowers its dark reflections.

That saying. Like water off a duck's back.

It's been weeks now. Government assurance that the clean-up is going better than planned.

Oil has its own slick intelligence and knows where to hide.


You used to ignore her news.

–She's old, you said. She complains. She has too much time to think alone. She broods.

Once you start to let her news in, it is a screaming around the edges of every story you hear.

The story is that oil can blend and bond and fit into the landscape it's given.

The story is that one thing leads to another.

The story is that the wind is spreading the oil. The coves that edge the islands, the inlets and harbours, take the oil in and keep it safe.

The story is that she is dying.

The story is that whales have likely developed a whistle in their dialect that means "oil."

The story, the environmentalist tells the camera, is that there is such a thing as the end of the world.

–So dramatic, she says to the TV (to you). Apocalypses are for queens. Stick to natural disaster. No point getting all dramatic.

–Drama's how he got on the news, you point out.

The environmentalist made the news for nearly a week by lying on a beach at the edge of the city, covered in oil.

–I thought that was a bit much, she says.

But she put the picture of him on the fridge. Every day for

a week a new photo of him — her fridge an evolving shrine. Volunteers poured oil on him from blown glass pitchers donated by a famous local artist. Every morning they poured the oil, head to toe. A ritual for the cameras to play before and after the morning weather. Sun lit the slant of oil as it met his skin. He was naked. His nakedness and the thick tongue of oil. The sunlight and the glass and his smile against bright sand. Shoulders sculpted in grease-black clay with devotional hands.

After a week, the oil company agreed to implement a twenty-million-dollar refurbishment project for the oldest freighters.

A politician was shown on the front cover of the newspaper drinking champagne from a pitcher.

–No respect, she said.

Now the environmentalist says apocalypse to the TV camera and she says fiddlesticks. You say nothing.

–And do you know, she says. I was around the last time the world ended and the last thirteen times before that. And nothing changed much then. So.

That's just the way she sees things, you think. Nothing will ever change because nothing ever has. Fatalistic logic, you've snapped at her.

In the satellite images, the coast darkens. The tide drags the oil out in a shallow semi-circle, across the back of the earth. You watch the screen and the ocean brings its own eclipse.


On some trips to the island where she lives, you stay in your car on the boat's lower deck. Dogs stare from windows. The smell of car exhaust and the ocean's mealy brine. The car deck is cold, an intertidal cave. When the water level drops, you will be on the island.

Her living room.

She clips articles about the spill. She fills the tray placed across her knees. The TV is a third person, conciliatory.

– Tell me a story, she barks.

– I don't have a story.

You sip the iced tea she made you. Sharp Moroccan mint from her balcony pots.

– You go around, you go out, you have a job, you have friends. You're young.

– I don't know. What kind of story?

– The Knowledge Network is more entertaining than you, she says. I don't know why you even come here if you have nothing to say.

That pisses you off. The boat ride is long. And expensive.

– So what, you say. You tell me a story. What about one of those apocalypses?

– Well which one. The first one. Or the eleventh.

She laughs.

– Are you making fun of me?

– No. You're my only visitor who comes on a boat. Boat visitors are the most important.

– Oh, fuck this.

She does what she never does: she picks up the remote and turns the TV off. She twists in her corduroy recliner to face you, to tell you.

– I'll tell you about the fourth apocalypse. This apocalypse happened beside the Black Sea. No pun intended, don't start with me. So an army came to the Black Sea. They said,

Everyone who belongs to Group x should send one man from their household to the harbour. This was a big harbour, it was used for trade. Everyone said, Why? Doesn't matter, the army said. They had lots of troops, so everyone listened. All the men from Group x were shot and then their bodies were piled on the shore of the Black Sea and they were burned. Then the army threw their bones into the ocean.

You look at her. She looks at the TV. She turns it back on.

–Why did you tell me that, you say.

She says nothing.


You do not take the boat to the island for three weeks.

She calls and leaves a message. Her voice on the machine rasps. Are you. Coming to the island soon.

She asks, When will I see you next?

The newspaper, she says, have you seen the paper today.

Even when you do not go to the island, she is telling you her news.

More whales, she says.

You go out and buy copies of the three papers she subscribes to. When you open the first paper to the centrespread, you see men instead of whales. Men on their knees, gushing smoke.

The rescue workers in their red jackets. Four black whales on a white beach. No one knows why. They couldn't find their way through the slick water, or did they stop breathing, or did they look for a place to be seen.

That's what she thinks.

So we can see what we're doing to them. Her voice on your machine.

You pick up the phone.

Don't be crazy, you say.

Good to hear your voice, she says.

If only the wind would stop. The oil siphoned out, one long dark thought. You would uncap your thumb and drain it some-where for safekeeping.

The faces of the whales. Unbelievably large. Exaggerated masks of sleeping men. Each whale contains a lot of oil, the articles say. The government is negotiating with the local First Nations about how to dispose of the bodies.

–One landfill apiece, she says.

The small mockery of a bird turning its sharp face.

–I don't even get the paper. I wouldn't have seen all of it.

–I thought you'd want to know, she says. She hangs up.

That's her. To call and call and then hang up.


You can't sleep.

Whales blaze under your eyelids. Whales awake and rush out of you. You sleep and wake up on a beach where white sand flows in small bright streams amongst the black. The whales and men are resting together. They are on fire. A whale turns and touches a man. The man opens his eyes. You wake up chok-ing, your mouth filling with your own water. Turn and heave it out, the hot salt breath of a whale spoiling from the inside. You dial her number. There's no one else you would call like this, your voice not ready as you punch out the numbers. The water that drains from your face.

–Hello?

–Why did you tell you me that story?

–You? It's so late.

–I can't sleep anymore. Not since you told me that story.

–I'm sorry.

–I just want you to know you —

–I'm sorry.

She sounds old.

–Will you come again, if I don't tell you any more stories?

You take the boat to the island.

The boat moves through morning, moves through evening, at the same speed every time. Every trip is exactly the same. Clam chowder from deep industrial pots, even at breakfast.

There is a safety drill. The voice on the PA system tells All Passengers Not To Be Alarmed, This Is Only A Drill. The passengers who've been zoned out on their iPods yank out their white earbuds and stare at the crew running and shouting methodically, knees bobbing. Toy soldiers. You don't tell the deaf passengers, this is only a drill. You need to watch them. Their leaning and wondering. What did I miss.

A man gets up and touches a crew member's shoulder. Frowning, uncertain.

You begin to laugh.

Your stomach aches, you're laughing so hard.

They glare at you.

You get up and hurry out onto the deck and look for the oil. It's gone now, or it was never here. Not gone, she's told you. Absorbed. When it's all inside, that's when it does the most damage. When it gets inside it starts its own changes.

You stand on the deck until it appears. The island.

You've seen this island all your life. She has always been on it.

You buy a cake.

The girl in the bakery puts the cake into a white box. Before pulling away from your apartment building, you put the seat belt over the box. The cake sits on the passenger seat. The seat belt keeps the cake perfectly still during the ride to the boat. On the boat to the island, you stay in your car on the lower deck.

Dense cake. Ganache, butter cream. A red ring of maraschino cherries, the kind she likes, the cheap kind. Fluorescent, fished from a bottle like the pickles she eats with fish.

–Pickles with fish, you sneered once. Gross.

–When you're old you'll want pickles with your fish. Your blood is salty like mine. That's why people like us will never be happy. We were incubated in pickling jars. Mistake at the hospital.

–Very funny.

A woman walks past your car, sees the seat belt around the cake box, and smiles at you and the cake box. When you begin to weep she speeds up. Her footsteps ring across the metal deck.

Gates. Steps. Clattering at the edges of things.

You unbuckle the seat belt and put the cake box on the floor.

At her apartment door you say, I brought a cake.

People who live in the building drop by all day. You are surprised she knows anybody in her building; she has never mentioned these people before. She plucks the maraschino cherries off and puts them in a small glass ice cream bowl for herself. She gives everyone a thick slice of cake until it's gone. Then she sits with the bowl in her hands and eats the cherries, one by one. Lips stained a false red. You've never seen her wear makeup.

–I should have just brought you a jar of cherries, you say.

–That would have been clever, she says.

–Next year I'll give you cherry pickles for your birthday. To eat with fish.

–This is my last birthday, she says.

–You don't know that.

–I do.

–No you don't.

–Alright, she says.

Two women who brought Chinese takeout look at you. Their smiles of gentle pity.

–Talking doesn't matter anyway, she says. She flips her hand at you, smiling. It's all just talk and talk and talk. Eat your dinner.

Later, you have missed the last sailing. Someone gives you a blanket.

You wake on her fifty-year-old couch, full of her old smell. A figure rushing water toward your eye. Coming through the corrugated grey light.

–You had a nightmare.

Her fingers pulling your hair straight. Your soaked hair. Her shadow cooling you. The small of your back throbbing, the small of her hand.

You shut your eyes to keep down the tide that draws the bones out of your body one by one.

–My mother told me that story, she says quietly. Now it's yours.

Her night cream, the stink of it, like clay and gasoline. A

smell you've hated since before your memory took solid form, her salt, her salt, you would drink it if you could.

You buy subscriptions to all three newspapers. The two national papers and the one for just here. You take her the pictures you clip out for her. Now that she can no longer see, now that she is blind as a beast in dark water. You cover her fridge with the pictures, the way she did. The welt shrinks, the oil pulls out of the inlets. It's still there, she mutters. White sand on the beach where the whales were found and the new stronger freighters. Same war, different weapons, she says. Yes, but it's something, you say. How you apologize for everything, try to make it better with words, and how this always makes you wrong. Something, she says. Something the way the tide is something, something the way a fish is something. She laughs. I don't understand, you say. You will, she says. But not until it comes back.

You go on the boat to see her. You come back. The next day a man calls you, an old friend of hers, the friend who gave you all that vodka at her birthday party.

Easily. No pain. In her sleep.

She leaves herself to you. Pickle jar. Screw-top.

You pour her into the ocean.

You don't need to go to the island today.

You have always gone to the island.

You don't need to go the island today.

You've gone to the island for many years.
You've come to the island for many years.
Don't go to the island today.
If you go to the island today.
You need to go to the island today.
No. You need to get some rest.
You need to get some rest.
The island will still be there when you wake up.
You don't need to go to the island tomorrow.
Tomorrow, the island.

# FACE

THAT SUMMER, we watched the houses on our block disappear.
One by one. The noise of construction filled everything. Bird-
song drilled holes in the clawing of the bulldozers.

The same for each house. The FOR SALE sign came down
and a crew arrived. Men in white T-shirts. The sweat made the
cotton transparent, made their muscles swim clearly. Mornings,
they stood on the curb, downing 7-Eleven coffees, dropped the
paper cups in the gutters. Then they started their machines.

We lived in the houses that remained. We travelled the street, a bright bicycle herd, hazing the dumpsters full of doors and walls that had belonged to the people who were now gone. Families moved to the wealthier neighbourhood up the hill or to the suburbs.

The crews came in their trucks and stayed, the months heating up, more houses selling.

The yards were razed and the old yellow cedars fell. Concrete slopped into the pits from the metal maws lowered from the back of trucks. White tanks rolled, growling harsh-bellied hunger. The foundation. Bolts and rebar. Then wood, rising.

The pale wood frame going up and the walls climbing it piece by piece. The sun cut a pattern of squares in our retinas as we watched. A new grid for our neighbourhood sky.

One of the oldest boys had slender glistening scars on his arms from an accident with boiling water. The burn marks flowed down his forearms, the way the water had travelled. He was the first to climb down into one of the pits. He waited until after dark one night.

He walked around for two days with what he'd found.

– You should see the shit that's just lying around down there, he said.

He held out the piece of bone he'd found. Nothing like bones I'd seen before. Nothing like a bone from a picture. This bone wasn't white. It was brown and crumbling at the edges, soft-looking, like wood. Another boy said it wasn't a bone, but everyone could see that it was.

The burned boy went back for more. He went down in the

pits again, taking his best friend, who played hockey by himself against his garage door every night, sending hollow metallic bursts down the block, so everyone knew at the same moment when his sweat got its first chill and he went inside; then we knew it was night.

–Check it out.

A brass doorknob, its side flattened like a rotten apple. Crescent moon of stained glass window. Another bone. This one longer. One girl held it up against her arm to see and we yelled at her. Gross! Don't do that! Our fear-torn laughter.

Cool stuff. Treasure. Parts of the pipes that dangled in the earth around the smashed-in houses like roots. Things we had known were there, in theory, but had never thought about handling, holding close and smelling. Comparing the way one kind of metal rotted with another. The rot of metal and the rot of bone. Someone turned and handed me a brick. Its edges were worn down: a red-brown ovoid, a warm speckled weight, resting on my palm like a dinosaur egg or a well-tumbled beach stone. I remember the number stamped into it: 1913.

A girl in our group decided we should start to keep the stuff. There was a tree beside her house. It looked like a regular tree from outside, she said, but inside there was a dry balloon-shaped room, a dirt floor that she swept every few days. Once she made the suggestion, it became our project for that summer. As the houses fell, we visited the pits, learning the striations of black and silver and white clays. A cool-shadowed underground world. Deep down, everything was wet, smelled of riverbed.

We all needed names. The girl who owned the tree was the

Chief Organizer. The burned boy who found the first bone was the Scientist. A short, red-headed kid from down the street who later became a local news anchor was named Second Royal Clerk. A future teacher was the Deputy Excavator. Imperial Lemonade Maker, who was too little for a real name. First Royal Clerk would end up in foster care two years later, bounce through high schools on the West and then the East side, and when I was nineteen or twenty I would see her on Granville downtown once, panhandling, her left arm across the back of a sunstroked German shepherd, and I would drop a five dollar bill onto her shoe but not say hello, doubting her consciousness, wanting her not to recognize me in return.

I already wrote everything down anyway so they made me Secretary.


Sunlight enters through the eye. Heat warps days. We slipped into the pits after dinner while our parents poached in their sweat in front of the televisions in the houses. We were all pulling on one hot net that dragged things up from the bottom. We had one eye cramped from looking, the light moving into all the hollow places the houses left, making the holes gleam.

Until the cement gushed down into each pit, everything belonged to us. We carried our finds back to the tree where the Chief Organizer organized the stash into rows, the Scientist inspected each object and I wrote an objective and accurate description of each object. I did this methodically, enjoying the satisfying stamp of each word, until we found Face.

When the old houses fell, each part fell heavily. Brick and hardwood floor. Obstinate chimneys. Stone fireplaces. Fathers salvaged chunks of granite and quartz for rock gardens and pathways. Houses built to last, my father said. Not made for this one demolition. We biked to our houses, wondering whose was next. Gutters snapped like kindling. The upended roots of trees snatched from the soil with a series of jerking metallic roars. The bulldozer, its wide-spaced teeth. The original trees, my father told me. The trees from before there were houses.

From before there were houses.

–Before the houses, was everything, just, trees?

My dad said he'd bought the house from another man who was from Saskatchewan. He didn't know.

–Ask your mother.

I asked her and she said the city had been here for a really long time. She reached out and felt my hair between her thumbs. Now I know what my mother did not say or know: that if you ask these questions the city begins to peel away at its edges.

They never noticed us. Our child-sized incursions. We were the raccoons and the cats, the smalls of night travel. Additional passengers.


Walls tipped inward. Demolition, my father called it. Fiasco, my mother called it. All the houses being ripped down and what's being built in their place, she raged, just boxes, blocks and blocks of beige boxes. Quick construction, my father agreed. That's why they're all the same — nod, nod, nod — you just do the same thing over and over and that's the fastest way to get it done. I nodded because that's what we were doing — standing in our kitchen, heating glasses of water with our hands, nodding. Nodding was a kind of conversation I needed to learn.

–Yeah, I said, all the stuff in all the construction sites is the same.

My mother turned. One finger arced outward.

–Stay out of the construction sites, she said. You could step on a nail and get an infection.

She and my father leaned into the window's lukewarm breath.

–Listen to your mother. You've got plenty of other places to play.

–You aren't going down there are you?

–No.

–You'd better not be.

–I'm not.

My mother sighed, heat escaping from between her lips. I didn't yet know that she was pregnant.

–Maybe we should move too.

–Maybe, my father said, but let's wait and see what the market does. It's this immigration jump, you know, that can't last forever. Things'll settle down.

Because of something that had happened in China, I'd heard vaguely from other kids' parents. I nodded, pretending to know. It was changing Vancouver, they said. That's why all the old houses were being knocked down. The new people didn't like old houses.

–The longer we hold out the more we can sell for, my father said.

I recognized his Voice of Reason.

–God it's just all the construction, the noise makes me crazy. All day long.

–They're putting in long hours that's for sure.

–It's too much. Don't they know people live here.

–The whole city's changing, not just here.

–I'm not staying here if I don't have any neighbours left.

This was the first time our leaving was mentioned. I had been born in that house. My mother palmed her stomach. My father refilled his water glass and handed it to her, shaking his head.


We were all there when Face came out of the earth.

Just before dark, but the sky blazed summer down on us. The clay at the bottom of the pit shone like snowblindness. This was the sixth, possibly the seventh pit we'd searched as a team.

The Scientist crouched, scratched at the grit around the openings — then the openings were eyes. Open eyes. He dropped his hands.

–Holy shit, he whispered.

We all backed away, then leaned in.

Never a face without its skin before. Skull, nose bridge, frail frame for eyes, blunt slope, someone's forehead.

–Shit it's a person, said the First Royal Clerk.

–What'd you think it was, God you're an asshole, said the Deputy Excavator.

–But it's the head.

–It has fucking eyes.

–It's looking at me, said the Imperial Lemonade Maker.

–What do we do with it?

–Shit be careful.

–Okay okay okay we need to get it back to the tree for in-spection, said the Chief Organizer. We always listened to her because she owned the tree.

Three boys slipped off their T-shirts, instinctively, silently, as if they were about to plunge into the ocean.

–Get the rest of the crud off.

We sat in a circle. The Scientist scratched with his finger-nails, stopped, rubbed hard with the side of his hand. He flipped her over. The back of her skull was gone.

–Where's the rest?

–They ate people.

–No one eats bones you fucking moron, said the Scientist.

–Stop swearing, said the Chief Organizer.

No one wanted to say anything else. Not in front of Face.

The Chief Organizer balled up one of the T-shirts and used it to stuff the back of the skull. The other two T-shirts she folded carefully around the eyes. I got one last glimpse before the navy blue Canucks T-shirt covered her up. Her teeth, worn down and strong, evenly spaced, nut brown.

My tongue flickered over my teeth, checked my own full set, swept swiftly from one side of my mouth to the other, while the Chief Organizer stood up, holding the bundle in her arms. We followed her back to the tree.


We tried to put her back together, but we couldn't. Construc-tion on the pit where we'd found her started after a week's delay. We couldn't tell anyone about her, now that everything had started. The concrete flowed in, hardened into a flat grey hardness. Foundation is a sealant.

The Second Royal Clerk got a book about skeletons from the library off Broadway. All kinds: horses, bears, cats, mice, and people.

We have about half of her, he said. The bones we'd found around her face spelled out half a body, some inevitable gaps.

We sketched out the rest of her body. Not tall. Not much taller than the tallest of us. We had part of a leg. A few ribs. A shoulder blade, its small hollow.

Laid out on the earth inside the privacy of the tree, pine needles swept out. Evidence of a makeshift woman. Someone had brought a broom from the apartment of an aunt who would never notice, because she didn't have a family.

–Secretary, write all this down. This is all really important.

Most important was the front of her skull. If we hadn't found Face we'd probably have forgotten about her and moved on to something else. As we had kept the first bone but not investigated it. It was something else crushed and left behind, part of the crushed leftovers, like everything else in our neighbourhood, now.

A father's leather jacket was stolen. Face was placed inside, the arms folded gently to cover the fragile eye sockets, the even eternal teeth. What had she tasted? Ears had grown outward from her head. Now they were gone. I felt my ears — prodded, thoroughly folded and felt my ears for the first time — and they were skin and soft stuff, cartilage, disposable texture that would vanished like the sounds they processed. How much of my body was a soft pulmonary plant? Eyes. Tongue. Ears. Only bones would stay, outline and skull. When we wanted to look at her, we unwrapped the weightless leather arms. When we'd all looked long enough, we folded the arms carefully around Face, so she could sleep.

One night, my mother spread a cold towel on my face and neck and I disappeared. My sunburned skin a hood to shed.

–Don't touch it, I screamed about my skin that cooked, then cooled, and replaced itself.

–You could get scars, my mother said.

–I don't care.

Now I knew that my skin could regrow. I liked how the burned skin looked. Red and petal-smooth.

We sat in a circle, Face in the middle.

We tried to name her.

–The name of our street: Mrs. Valley.

–You can't call her that, she's not married.

A few girls called her Grandma.

Some boys called her Head-Like-A-Basketball.

–So not funny.

I called her You.

She didn't answer. I watched her. One day I would catch her looking back. She listened, did not hear, saw everything, had emptiness for eyes, had lost her eyes to the earth, had eyes but they were only outlines, rather than the pale lamps of our eyes, glowing anxiously in the tree's sheltering half-world.

–Shit. You think she was a kid? asked the Admiral of 7-Eleven, who almost never spoke.

I felt my stomach touch itself, weak and hot.

– No, I can tell she was old, I said.

– But there's no skin. My mom says you can always tell age from skin.

– God you're stupid.

– How do we know it's a girl?

– Yeah you're right. It could be a guy. It's just bones.

– She was old, I said. She was really old.

– What? How do you know?

– She told me.

– You're the Secretary, said the Scientist, turning to me, his voice hard and soft. You're supposed to be objective. He pointed at me and I wrote down vengefully, *as his asthma bracelet rattled*, even though it was too delicate to make a sound.

– Stick to the facts.

I nodded and pretended to review the notes I had taken at this meeting, so the Chief Organizer and Scientist wouldn't doubt my reliability. The role of Secretary had become important to me, the first role I'd had in a group that I felt was really mine. In the fall when we went back to school, I would have no role with its own name, and I sucked at sports.

Now, when I reread the notes I took that summer, I see the careful detail, the shorthand I developed for names and expressions. The drawings I made of Face, my clumsy hand recording ovoids and the side-penciled cheeks. A cramped list entitled Cause of Death that we made as a group.

Drowned in ancient ocean that used to be here.

Killed by a bear.

Really old.

Killed by someone else (war?).

Bow and arrow.

Just died, it happens.

And we could never decide on a name so we just called her Face.


My bedroom was in the basement of our house. Easy to climb out. Window ledge kissed grass. I ran across the lawns dampened by the darkness, moved swift and soundless, toetips on ice.

There were things I wanted to tell her. Everything I wasn't allowed to put in the official notes.

I sat cross-legged. The huge ticking silence of the tree and the wide street beyond it made me breathe loud, hard, to fill some space. She lay in front of me on the folded leather jacket.

– The house that was on top of where you were was Mrs Cornwall's, I told her. Her husband died because he drank too much. She tried to kill herself so she's in the hospital and her son sold the house so that's why it got knocked down. I'm not supposed to know. She's seventy-three years old. I think that's really old for someone to try to kill herself. My dad said some people just can't take it anymore sometimes. You just never know about people.

– Everything in the neighbourhood's being torn down, not just your house. There's lots of people coming from China. It's called the Asian invasion. Just because Asia's where they're coming from. Is it OK for me to touch you?

I accepted her silence as permission.

I'd never been able to feel her properly with the others around. The bone was not cold like I expected, the cold of bone, but a neutral temperature, the temperature of wood or sun-dried grass. I rested my hand very lightly on her. I knew that she was the oldest thing I had ever touched. How old are you? I'm seven. She didn't answer. I took my hand away.

–So you're probably wondering why I'm here.

My voice rang false; I was being too formal. But this is what my mother had taught me to do: in an awkward moment in a conversation, say why you wanted to talk to the person and then say thank you and then say goodbye.

–I think you deserve to know what's going on. We've been looking in the other pits every day and we haven't found anything else like you.

I looked at my hands.

–I'm the Secretary. They don't want me to tell you this. You're the only one. Maybe other bones, but those are just little bits. I don't even know. I'm sorry.

It had been a few weeks since we'd found Face and only: bent red nails, date-stamped bricks, glass.

–What are you doing?

For a second I thought the voice had come from her. I scuttled back on my hands and heels. But it was a male voice, a live voice, because hers would be gentle-edged and low. I knew her sound already, could hear it clearly. (I can still remember, now, precisely, the sound of Face's voice.) Then I looked up and saw him.

The Scientist stood in the tree's green shadowcore.

–What are you doing here?

–What are *you* doing here?

–I come every night. It's part of my job.

–It is?

–Yeah. Why should you know? You're just Secretary.

He walked forward, stepped in front of Face, blocking me from her.

– What were you saying to her?

– Nothing.

– You better tell. Or I'll kick you out of the project.

– I was just talking to her.

For a moment he looked frightened. I noticed that he was carrying a blanket under his arm. I wondered how often he slept here. Why didn't his parents notice and stop him? He noticed me staring and held the blanket behind his back, then dropped it and kicked it aside.

– Did she say anything?

– It's a secret.

The Scientist laughed.

– Yeah right.

– I told her everything.

– Like what?

– Like we've been lying to her.

– Bout what?

– We're not going to find anything else like her.

He shrugged and his anger seemed to drain into the smoothness of his voice.

– So what? She's bones. You talked to a bunch of bone. So what.

He laughed.

– You're only seven, he said.

– So?

– I'm twelve, okay? Everything's not such a big deal.

– She's a person.

– Shut up.

–I want to go home.

–Be quiet.

–I want to go home!

I ran forward and he moved into my path. He waved his arms angrily. He was huge. I remember looking up, his burn scars climbed higher in the dim light. Pale, reaching. Unimaginable smoothness of the scars, his arms, reaching.

Then, gripping both my wrists, his fingers light and hard, slim vices. Leaned in, the heat of his face.

–Look. It's all a big fucking game, okay? A big fucking game. So just get over it now. Talk to her all you want but it won't make any difference. You wanna know what she is? You won't read it in any history book because they don't teach it in school. The truth is people like us killed all of them and that's just the way history works. Okay? Okay? Okay? Now you know. Put that in your notes. You'll be a lot happier when you learn not to give a shit about things.

Nobody had ever told me how his water burns had happened and I didn't wonder about the story until then. He released my wrists and I stopped crying.

I watched him kneel and fold the arms of the leather jacket around Face and restore her to her place in the collection.

The Scientist hooked his long arm around my shaking back and walked me home across the silent lawns.

Halfway across the third lawn he murmured, I'm sorry.

We had all been trained in sorries and acceptances.

–I accept your apology, I said.

It soothed, this small ritual.

He knelt beside my bedroom window and pushed it gently inward so I could slip back into the sleeping house, set my feet on the chilled floor of my room, far below the sloping shoulders of the shingled roof, which I did not know would fall within the year, the same as all the others.

The Scientist was the next to go. The FOR SALE sign stayed up for two days.

His family did not move to another house. The Scientist went with his father to an apartment downtown. His sister went with his mother to Alberta. He did not come to the tree after the FOR SALE sign went up on his lawn. We knew that he was already gone, a ghost breathing in his basement bedroom. The 1913 brick disappeared from the collection. Then one of Face's ribs. We let these things go without mention.

A week after the moving vans full of his family's things pulled away, the Scientist's house was pulled down. We descended into the pit. Its shadowed vertical playground. We found a piece of copper and a black stone the size of a fist, carved with the fins of a whale.

I wrote in my notebook: They had an ocean.

We put the copper and the whale with Face, to keep her company.

Three days later:
—Someone told.
—Who?
—Someone. Dunno. Doesn't matter.
—Who told?
—Shit. Why'd he tell?

–Don't know.

–Who?

–Doesn't matter who!

–They know now so who cares.

–Why'd someone have to tell.

–But she's ours.

–Finders keepers.


All of our parents. Pale hoop of faces. The bones laid in the centre of the coffee table with the skeleton library book (water-stained, green tree juice-stained, long overdue), the stained glass shards, the doorknobs, and Face.

One father reached out and touched Face's left eye socket. My mother winced. Then looked at me.

–Do we know how long this has been going on?

–It was under the Cornwall house.

–God. More than a month. God. Half the summer.

–The Cornwall house. Did anyone call the son?

–I don't have his number.

–Did Linda know?

–How could she have?

A mother I'd hardly seen before, a mother with a job and a work haircut, rested her glass of white wine on her knee and said, You know what happens if this gets out? They dig up everyone's yards.

–What?

–Yes.

–No. What?

–Look, she said. A friend of mine's a lawyer and she dealt

with a case like this. This is a partial skeleton. There could be more. Who knows. So it'll be a big deal. There'll be a dig, it'll be in the news. And in BC, if they find an Aboriginal, um, site, um, remains, on your property, you pay for the excavation. It's in the law.

–How much?

–The couple my friend represented coughed up thirty grand.

–We don't have that kind of money.

–No one's putting a fucking land claim on my yard.

–You wouldn't have much of a choice, would you.

–I've never heard of that law.

–We bought this house with our own money. No one said anything about that law.

–Should we be talking about this in front of the kids?

The Chief Organizer started crying, quietly, into her hands.

The rest of us sat mutely, cross-legged, watching our parents go wild.

My mother turned to us.

–Why couldn't you just have left it alone. Why couldn't you just have left it there.

–OK. Let's try to just stay calm, let's just try to talk about this in a, uh, calm way.

–Calm? This is a hell of a lot of money we're talking about.

–It's the Campbell house not ours for God's sakes. And the new house is already built and sold. What're they going to do, knock down the new one too?

–They will if we report this.

–To who?

Silence.

–Well. I don't know. It's the law, that's what I know.

–This neighbourhood's ruined anyway.

–Don't say that.

–Well, look. Whatever we do we all have to do the same thing. Because if they find stuff on one site, they'll have to look around. The bones and the, uh, carving, came from different places you said, right, Elizabeth?

The Chief Organizer nodded miserably. I had almost forgotten her real name.

–We're putting our house on the market next week. It's all arranged.

Face lay on the coffee table. I watched her.

The Chief Organizer's father put his hand on her shoulder. Sweetie, he said, we need to know everything that's happened so we can make a decision.

The Chief Organizer smeared tears across her cheeks. She pointed at me.

–She's the Secretary. She wrote everything down.


From my notes they determined most of what had happened. The collection was re-organized on the coffee table and matched to the descriptions and sketches. My mother turned and repeated to me, Why didn't you just leave it?

Someone else's mother put a hand on my mother's arm.

My mother shook her head.

–I'm pregnant, she said. We need a bigger house. I can't deal with this.

The Chief Inspector's father nodded.

–Almost all of us are moving, aren't we? So this doesn't really matter, does it.

–I'm sorry, the Chief Organizer sobbed, it was just a game.

–It's okay, sweetie, her mother said, rubbing her back.

–No harm done, someone's father said. Another father made a joke about us being aspiring paleontologists. Pretty young for summer school. Everybody laughed. I took my father's hand and squeezed his fingers together until he looked down at me. What? he whispered. I breathed into his ear: Don't let them take her. He maintained his rigid yearbook smile, shook his head, still looking straight into the centre of the adult laughing faces. Stop it, he mouthed.


We kept Face. After moving into a house in another neighbourhood, my mother took Face out of a box marked DELICATE and hung her over the cedar mantle above our new fireplace. An imposing, sculptural fireplace made of granite, one of the reasons my mother had chosen this house. The collection had been distributed to the families. A bone for each family.

It was the right thing to do, my father had told me. Throwing it all away just hadn't felt right. My mother and father told me over dinner that it was over. No one would do anything. Everyone agreed. All the other children too. I was the last one. We would all just move on. It would be for the best. Forget.

Face watched from the mantle — watched my younger brother arrive, then a sister, then another brother. They didn't know the story and I didn't tell them. The summer we had taken Face out of the earth and the other parts of her body faded from me, bright and vague as everything under that demolition summer's light. The dark and cool of the clay pits, the houses that covered everything over.

When I moved away for undergrad my mother asked me if I wanted anything from the house to take with me to my dorm room. The face above the fireplace, I said. She stared and said, The skull? Why do you want that? You asked me what I wanted, I said. She said, I've been planning to take it into the museum at the university, the anthropology museum, for years, I've just never gotten around to it. I nodded. Good, I said. I packed my clothes and books The night before my flight I lay on my bed. I thought, this is my last night in this house. This is the last night I will live in this house. I walked up the stairs into the living room. In the darkness I could see Face hanging above the fireplace. The shell-grey light coming through the large windows. She had not changed, she would not change. I had not looked at her carefully for years. I walked to the fireplace and took her down from her hook. Touched her all over for the first time since that night in the tree when the Scientist had held my wrists and screamed the truth down my throat. She looked and felt exactly the same. No temperature. Lightweight. She had hung over our fireplace for ten years. I put Face in my backpack, wheeled my bike into the alley, rode my bike down the hills of the city to the beach. I carried her into the water, holding her up. The ocean a shock of cold at every inch, August fleeing from the waves and tomorrow it would be September and I would be on the plane going east. The water at my shoulders, I threw Face outward and I did not wait to see where she went under.

# SWIMMERS

**HE FALLS ASLEEP** on a beach in the city's elbow and night blows newspapers over him. In the morning rain has soaked yesterday's newsprint across his forehead, yesterday's news. Dawn is happening. First light on water, first ink.

Sidewalk unrolling there to stumble up, away from the Pacific. Back up the street past all last night's doors. Kids across the street, parallel lines pointing the way to school, jackets in every primary colour, shouting morning.

Just dance. Club darkness muggy with liquor breath, ice cubes snapped between teeth and under rhythmed feet, bare shoulders like lit fish teeming the crowd's surface. Faces press into the glass of each other. Who are you? Come near me. Get away. He dances like a third-grader, like a sexbot, like a snake charming another snake. Jump up, flap arms, shimmy down and move your butt, every slut since Chaucer knows that move.

Dark early morning/midnight. Rain hurtles down gutters toward the ocean. He breathes himself out into the chill air, a clove-scented cloud following the street to the water. This is where he comes after everything every day is done.


The first time she sees him. Shoulders like a tall river-hunting bird, eyes trapping fish thoughts. Black hair swinging low. His laugh, making a crack in the sounds of traffic. He lies on the curb laughing, a body like wires thrown down on the road by a windstorm, electricity startling his arms and legs, hurling back the bodies of others.

She sees him most nights in the places they both go.

On the balcony above the crowd, looking down at the bodies swinging together, they rest and drink and watch the dancing ocean, heads and arms tossed into light.

–Why are they all here?

–Fashion, fun, drinking, sex, nothing.

They become a familiar creature. This strange space that will keep them together.

This season sidewalks make glistening land bridges between seas of yards and streets, cement and metal and plastic signs, and everybody in the city waits for sunlight, waits to surface.

Every night, they meet at the same corner. They dive into a dancing crowd again, again, but each wave of music pushes them back to where they began. She does not think of her classes that feel like bloodletting, the dimming eyes of her daylight friends. Outside, dark-veined rain lifts up the city's lights.

Take my hand, turn me round. Nightworld, forest of glinting dull-eyed buildings, this nightwood. They spill out onto another street. The ocean glowing at the end point of the gutter's slope, the moon's turned bright stone.

They don't talk to each other about their lovers. She goes to bed with a girl in one of her classes. It feels like the swell around a smoothed-out knot on driftwood, a strong turn of bone between two of her fingers and smoothness shouldn't be mistaken for softness. Her body something long and turning between her palms, something loose, rope-like. She holds her hard, a surprised face freezing in the air, like that, between reliefs. It is something.

He goes to the park beside the ocean. Men slide among the quiet trees. Their chests reflect light, the smoothness of the urban lake in the distance, dark mirror littered with crisp, curling leaves.

He guides her eye with one extended finger.

–All the people in my world are crazy, see?

Laughing, face stretched and turning through rye-rinsed glass.

–The guy at the all-night gourmet french fries place, the one with the cute/robot voice, he's crazy, see? This is what it's like when you live at night.

He has a job during the day but she doesn't know what and she doesn't ask. Her days of classes, students in rows, faces turned to the blank light. When she mentions class his face smooths with disinterest or lack of recognition. She is surprised to discover how simple it is to slice off nights from days, light from dark. How easy to double up on silent living, hold one hand beside the other without touching.


–Shit what was that sound?

A wave of crashing on the pavement, a piece torn off the sky.

–A car just went through the window of that store. Right through that huge window.

A busy street but pedestrians sidestep, keep moving, their voices and the horns of other cars rising in chorus. The driver stumbles off unharmed with his phone pressed into his ear, a gash like a red feather pressed to his forehead.

She takes a picture of her dancing partner posing glum-faced with the fresh wreck. Metal dug out and twisted. In the image stored in her phone: an astronaut posing with his stranded craft, street moonscape cratered with starlight, street light. This is her only evidence, she thinks.

A man sprints down from the apartment above the store and a shy cornered fire is smothered as instantly as it started.

He points at the crowd coming out of the Blenz at midnight. Students slope down the oil slick street. Jeans like denim leggings. Earmuff headphones. Briefcases moulded around laptops. Shoulderbagsipodsleathertinybuttonsplansplansplans.
 – Robots.
 – What makes a person not a robot?
 – That line between capacity and ability.

Just dance. How much can happen in what amount of time? How they fall into the folds, surf the edges for months, not wondering.

· · ·

Dancers flee from heavy bass like birds sensing a thunderstorm. Monsoon season in Vancouver. Busses are hired boats, nosing flooded corners and river bends posted with newspaper boxes, moving rows of picture windows of faces soaked with the future months of water, dark with the knowledge of their collective slow drowning.

Before, she had a theory she doesn't believe in anymore. All-encompassing adolescent invention. Hit her in high school physics class. Looked up to the blackboard on a day late in winter, glassy classmate faces stained opal, and saw it there, a phrase from the clouds: Particles of energy exist on different levels and their travel between is untraceable. The same goes for people, she thought.

Thinking a round trap. Minds are winding or they are still, brain quiet as burping frogs in a wet ditch. What is between this dug-up turning and women with taped-on smiles riding all the busses splashing up water wings from the gutters? She saw it then — no belief in epiphanies, just in fossil selves coming up under the skin, the blank levels people walk on, rows and rows and rows.

Now, she stares into the open darknesses between buildings, bodies, days. She could be pulled into those spaces, a body disappearing.


–Get that heart off your sleeve. Be more scary-lady, more regal-trashy, more you.

–Diana Ross, Jane Fonda with caterpillar drag queen eyebrows.

–Celine Dion as a crypt keeper, waltzing with a mannequin.

–Would you stop it with the references?

–I think I need a lobotomy while I sculpt dead air.

Just dance. Impulse over awkwardness. Fascination. What will the body do without thought? Pull in liquor like spacemen drinking nozzle-mouthed air, glass-faced, music lifting bodies from this blind floor. Underworld trappings. Nothing more cliché so turn off all the lights.

–I'm tired of the helplessness of desire of everyone around me.

–Don't pigeonhole people.

–People. Pigeons in their holes.

They dive into the ocean at the foot of the street. He sees her body moving away from his, a radiant thick fish. Through strong water, she is a dancer under black light. She sees him swept, close and far. She slips under. He floats nearby, his skin faded blue and his eyes flashing ciphers, and he raises his arms and gyrates, his limbs slowed by the weight of water. She looks upward. Here, seen from underwater, the city hangs from its concrete roots. Reflections of buildings dangle from the surface, windowed spears, entering her eyes as she swims upward toward the air of the world. It is raining and the raindrops wash the salt from her eyes, burn the world new.

Windows of late-night workers, dull white squares in the sky, spreadsheet star chart. The dark rooms they move through, music coming out of the bouncing floor, the floor moving like a chest, the heart inside it a drum under the floorboards, old hard beat. Music pushes up through her muscles, works them until they hurt and pulse with waterfisted rhythm.

He shouts over the sound.

–When I'm too old to come to these places, I'll get married. Ice sculptures, martinis and silver body paint.

They walk into the rain like seals underwater, water parting around their bodies, preordained paths in the thick airborne wet of this city.

She sweeps a hand at his dark-eyed bravado.

–No, you'll marry a boy with a dog and gym shorts on Sundays. All of Canada will join you at the lake.

She finds him outside a club, crying against a brick wall about an older lover who said, I only wanted to be good with you, then disappeared into the dancing bodies, the lights and small glasses flashing. Who is he? She asks him. How long was he with the lover? He shakes his head, shrugs, because there are relationships that come and go, fade and appear but are always there, are untraceable in the paths they work. She does not know him at all, she knows.

  – People will say anything to get to you.
  – Anything if that's what they want: you.
  – Can't give yourself if you don't.

Mornings. Lawn mowers hunt at her basement suite windows, crawl up like metalheaded mice. Thrum of waking eyelids. Just waiting for night again, gnawing for darkness, headaches the colour of sunlight, stretching the curtains to keep the brightness out. Spring starts. Everywhere sunlight, a common insult, shameless sparkle. But still the rain. He sings: You come and go, you come and go. Mantra of the undecided.

– I can't do this anymore.
  No beginning for this. Falls like a black bird shot out of the windowed sky.
  – What do you mean?
  – I'll stop thinking and will be ordinary.
  – I don't know. I'm the same.

She always knew he was held together by the tinsel that glitters at the corners of his eyes when excited or breaking. People with sturdy reassurance scrape her deep as the thickness of a fingernail.

She staggers into light-footed ground. She watches the club's searchlights sweep his chameleon skin, colours flashing through smoke like a weather system working out its hurricane core.

. . .

The top half of the province is burning, the bottom half is sliding into the sea, the part above that is melting. This is always the way the weather ends, they say it in all three newspapers.

He watches her slide between beats thrown off the ends of the DJ's fingers. She is his guest from the daylight hours, fallen through the trap door. Where did she come from and when will she leave? They gather shooters on the bar near their dancing, amber, honey-brown, orange, a collection of fireflies trapped under glass.

She waits for him on their corner, in all the usual places. She hasn't seen him for six nights, a width of wordless nights.

No rain tonight.

Fog ghosts rub their white bellies on the black streets.

She watches the dancers, silent traffickers of shadow and light, lovers without lovers. She looks for him down by the ocean.

The Pacific moves out there, a separate black planet. Sound of a broom sweeping the sky clean of its hard sharp stars. Top layer of water moving on and off, dark eyelid for the shining day of water.

He told her once that instead of paying for taxis some early mornings after dancing he fell asleep in the sand, stretched against a log, invisible from the street above. Once a newspaper blew over him and dew soaked it against his skin, printing the cheap ink onto his cheek, a direct transfer tattoo. He told her how he crouched in the surf and washed off yesterday's head-lines, walked to his job damp, head spinning with fading liquor and the waves that pounded on last night's washed-up bed.

She walks slowly among the logs, calling his name, morning birds chirping angrily at the human racket.


Spinning in the darkness of static/rain. The sparks from blown-out speakers hit wet skin like fireflies and stars and bodies swim together. Her limbs move slowly underwater. She does not know what it is for anymore, listening to her thoughts like the heartbeats of other people.

It is exhausting to be a chameleon, it's a headache to wake blue and sleep green, to eat yesterday's words and to not know the next day's. She does not know what that will be, what she is now.

Now she knows how to do tricks with her skin. This is what she learned from him. An allergy to one temperature of air, a witness protection program for the other person living inside. Where did he come from and where did he go?

That brightness from before what was that. Darkness now. Moods, cold water tickling long fingers down, looking for something in weather.

When we dovetail darkness like this we can't get away. Why he plunged when she did. Made a space in her, a small cave in the corner of her foot, too out-of-the-way to be worn down by leaving.

She climbs the stairs through darkness to the balcony above the dance floor and watches through her glass, looking for him. The bodies below, vertical, hands swinging, dogs swimming through rough water.

She sees him once in daylight:

Holding a pocket thesaurus open in one palm, flipping the waxy pages, fingers flickering like a water wheel. She always thought it was a joke, what he said about himself: Barstar to bookstore. The fluorescent lights, off-white linoleum, neat dark lettering, worlds packed in volumes placed in rows and rows around him. His face resting, eyebrows up, arch dandy put-on. His patchwork jacket and dark-rinse jeans. His cheeks the pale tenderness of a fish's soft underbelly. Inked shadows under his eyes. A creature pulled from the bottom of a shining tank and left on carpet. She watches him, fingers skimming spines of bestsellers gold-and-cerulean-thriller-blue, and knows that she is saying goodbye. She is saying goodbye to her friend.

He strides toward an exit, the PA system barking news of the summer's coming bargains. The spinning rack of bestsellers she hides behind, gold-and-purple covers, metal branches, a wild indoor tree, but any shelter is good enough.

Leave it like oil on a wet road. All the people passing through this life will smear and press in the old bloodlet stuff, it will be a stain on her skin she can only see when she traces its edges with her fingers. Don't dare to try, she tells herself, don't make it spread and shimmer. There is nothing after blacklung bitterness, the only thing is what to do after and after. Capture a daylight lover. Things quickly change away from here.

Morning streets and rain has washed all the city's ink away.

# GHOST STORIES

**TOGETHER WE LEAVE** the truck and walk into the first forest.

Where the undergrowth is too thick, out swings his machete and branches fall like hair. I slip on roots embedded in the mud, grey and round as veins coming out of the earth. He bends and hauls me up. Western light plummets through the canopy. Radiant white columns among the old growth. This is virgin forest, he told me during the long ride out in the hot truck, which means it's never been logged. These trees have been here for as long as there have been trees here.

I didn't even giggle at the word "virgin." I want to show him that I'm worth being brought here, just us.

–Was sure it'd be here. Before the road turns. Yeah that was the right road, sure of it.

He says this, stamping ahead of me like a bear.

My pant legs are slick from walking. I strip huckleberries from a branch, cover my mouth in a smash of red pulp.

–It maybe wasn't even the right road?

He sweeps his machete into the bush to his left, steps into the door cut out by the blade, and he's gone.

–Wait here, the voice he leaves behind says.

The forest drums with steady dripping. A squirrel corkscrews up a cedar, flashing a pattern to the roof of the forest. Then it's gone too.

–Uncle Frank.

The forest takes my whole voice, gives back nothing.

He read a book about the towns that were abandoned after the mining boom and we're going to find them. All the way here in the truck from his town, he told me what we will see. Empty streets and general stores in the middle of the forest. Skulls wearing wide-brim hats. He's lived on this part of Vancouver Island all his life and he recognised all the places in the book. The big mountain with the smile-shaped rock shelf in its side. The heart-shaped hollow of chanterelles. He knows all the roads. Marked and unmarked. How far all of them go.

–Uncle Frank.

–This way.

The side of his machete glows like part of a moon, a pale

green moon, the forest's own. We move faster now.

–Walk careful. We're in the middle of fucking nowhere. You fall, I'll have to carry you to the truck on my back.

–I read in science class that women have better pain tolerance.

Ferns lash my knuckles with their dripping ridged tongues.

–There's tonsa stuff I can't say around you that I could say around a boy.

–Like what?

–Can't say

He laughs, never looks at his feet. I force myself not to look down, to walk like him, as if I've memorised the ground's stones and roots. I fall and my lips press into leaves smooth and moist as skin.

–Watch out, little girl.

His muscled arms hoop my waist and I fly far up and land on the rubber muscle of his laughter, pounding my back.

–Let me down let me down let me down.

He swings me, releases me. My feet break through bracken, into mud thick as poured concrete, push through into the water under everything.

–Come on get going.


We come out under a logging road, a deep cut across a hill's pale belly. The clear-cut around the road has shown all of the hill's guts to the sun, left them to dry and blow, except for the scrap the loggers gathered into piles he calls honeypots.

–Must be a new road. They been all up in here the last month or so. Fuckers.

He points at the honeypots.

–Lookit all the wood they're goin to burn up. Burn it all up.

A piece of metal sticks out of the ground and he kneels and scrapes the machete against its surface, as if he's shaving meat. The metal extends past his shoulder, a thin line pointing the way to the hill.

–The old railroad. Knew it was here.

–There was a railroad here?

–You think they carried out the stuff mined on their backs?

–So is the ghost town over that hill?

–First we find the old railroad, then the town.

He kneels, runs a finger over the metal, bends right down and sniffs it.

–Lot of it's gone now. This piece ain't that long.

–Did it rot?

His laughter smacks off the scraped hill.

–Metal don't rot. Shit you're dumb sometimes. Gonna snow later.

He fingers the rail. Dark and worn, like a piece of old bone. He presses gently, feeling for a beat or for warmth.

–So?

–Shoulda put your jacket on in the truck. You get sick, you'll fuck up our day and your mom'll kill me.

–You're in shorts.

His legs are always tanned, even in winter. It's all the years walking around in the bush that does it, I think. Dirt under his skin. Dry stuff in his blood.

He walks past me, back into the forest, his machete swinging in his hand, a metronome flashing a message back to me through the trees. I am hypnotized by its swinging, stand and

watch time pass, then, stunned, I run after him into the sound
of water.

He never cuts more than one path. A few years ago, when he
first started taking me with him on rides, I told him that using
his machete in the forest was cruel. He said that if you don't cut
down much, it'll all grow back in a few months, that humanoids — that's what he calls people — fuck up the bush so much
with bulldozers that a few little paths don't matter.

–Don't know how anybody can sleep in a city. Humanoids
should be more like deer.

Back in the truck, he covers the wheel with maps. Pencilled
notes, dates of trips, where he's seen black bears and eagles,
road conditions, how many logging trucks, how big their loads
were. Logging trucks have right of way, always. They made these
roads. When the trucks roar by, I look out my window at their
teetering log pyramids.

He takes a Mountain Dew out of the cooler behind the seat.
I grab one too.

–That one mine, too?

–No.

–Stop that. Jeez you're scaring me. What an ugly, scary face
on a little girl.

He starts the motor and the road opens out to wild gold
grass, the ocean nodding over the trees. He slurps his Mountain Dew, lets out belches like the trombones in beginner band,
jerking the steering wheel to avoid the rocks in the road. He

calls the stones niggerheads, a word my dad told me I can't say. Niggerheads. Niggerheads. Niggerheads. Logger word. Island word. The logging company doesn't smooth out these roads; they're only used until all the trees in a part of the island are all gone. Then more roads are built somewhere else and the bushes and people like him fight for the old roads.

–Is your mom crazy?

Panic starts in my belly.

–I dunno. You mean crazy lady crazy or *crazy* crazy?

–Crazy crazy.

–Dunno. What do you mean.

When she's angry, I'm inside a house with no stairs. Just floors and floors. I ride down the steep hill near our house with my legs up, ankles out, pedals kaleidowhirling, and I want her to run out of the house just in time to see a car smash me in sideways.

I tilt my head back and raise my arm so the Mountain Dew falls in a long stream and babbles when it hits the pond in my mouth.

–Stop that. You know how much this truck cost?

–How much?

–Less than your spinal operation if you spill that.

I stick my nose into the can and smell the Mountain Dew because he smelled the piece of railroad. He does that kind of thing. Tastes the water on leaves. Licks his finger and sticks it up to feel the wind. Kicks bear turds open.

Berries. We're near where they're eating these days. This way instead then.

–I seen your mom screamin at your dad. I never yelled at Barb that bad and I met her when I was sixteen.

I stare at him, nervous. How much did he see?

–So? Maybe you guys're just boring.

–Bein borin's not bein not crazy.

–You've lived here all your life. That's pretty boring.

He jerks the wheel to the side, pushes down on the gas. I see a rocky slope looming, the bottom piece of the sky fading into a fan of trees. I scream.

Grinning, he pulls the truck back onto the road and drives on, the same as before, rumble steady, frozen light coming off the ocean. Nothing all the way to Japan, he told me once.

–Boring's actin like you're in the fuckin circus.

He doesn't say this until a few minutes later.

I get up on my knees on the seat, hold my can of Mountain Dew out the window and pour it out. He bellows. I take his can of Mountain Dew from the padded cup holder and stick the top half of my body out the window. He's yelling.

–You're crazy like your mom. Get back in the fuckin truck.

I smile back at him. My ears torn open by wind. I am crazy like her. Doing this for no reason, loving how much he hates it.

When my parents scream at each other in the kitchen, my mom always ends up forcing my dad out onto the deck, slamming the glass sliding door shut to keep him out in the cold. Once I walked in for a glass of milk during one of their fights and saw my dad on the porch, beating his fists on the glass. He was yelling but all I could hear was one word, again and again.

–In. In. In.

She stood on the warm side of the glass, drinking a cup of tea. The cup floated in the white light coming through the glass, just under his red face, steaming.

The rushing air lifts the stream of Mountain Dew, bends it

like a string of yellow-green cheap necklace pearls. I watch it waver behind us, then splash into the truck's side, each drop exploding one by one, breaking like frail glass.

There's something wrong with her but I don't know what.

–Get back in here. Just get back in here. In the truck. Come on. Okay, now.


When we stop, he skids down the bank to a stream and comes back with a soaked rag, wipes the Mountain Dew off, moving the rag in circles so it won't leave streaks.

–Why'd you do that, crazy girl? Go wash out the rag.

I cross my arms so he puts the rag on my shoulder and walks away.

When I get back from the stream, he holds up each arm of my jacket as I slip into it.

–See? I'm a gentleman.

–You look like a logger.

I say it because it's the worst insult I can think of.

He shrugs. His shoulders roll like water, drop hard.

–I been a logger for a while when I was round nineteen.

–Lying.

–Went into jobs on a tiny plane that jumped around and every guy threw up.

–Every guy? Yeah right.

–The floor of that plane was a lake of barf.

–Sick.

–That's all they got in China. So polluted they got lakes full up with barf.

–Lying.

–I seen it on TV last week. That's what's gonna be here too.

–Like when?

–Couple hundred years.

–So what then?

I worry all of a sudden that he's forgotten why we came.

–Ghost town!

–Don't crap yourself. I got the map here. You think it's north or south?

–I dunno.

–They said you was smart.

–*Were* smart not *was* smart. Too bad you didn't finish high school.

–North or south?

He puts his arms around his round junk-food stomach, the only part of him that isn't muscle.

–North.

Shakes his head, blue eyes faking mournful.

–Wrong. Dead north from this point, little girl. Let's go.

He takes the machete from behind his seat, zips up his windbreaker, and drops cans of Mountain Dew, shrinkwrapped pepperoni, O'Henry bars, half a loaf of bread, his maps, and the ghost town book into his backpack. He thinks, then drops in his flashlight.

We walk into the second forest.


This forest is different from the first. No rain. I miss the sound of water, the tick-tock of a watery clock buried in the mulch. The light here thinks and shifts, pale browns and greys, the colours of the birds who dance around the glass feeders on his porch back in town, where he melts Kraft cheese onto steaks on the barbecue and shoots his BB gun at the cats who stare from the leaning fences, their slanted eyes shimmering, starving. He's a soldier for the island birds. The birds that were brought in from England a hundred years ago that he says steal from the island birds, he leaves for the cats.

–You said it'd be close.

 –What you gonna do? Turn back?

 I'm going to turn back. I'm going to find the truck and figure out how to drive it back to the town where my mom and dad are drinking ginger ale and arguing with my relatives about the price of gas and whether it's safer to live in a city where there're more police or in small towns where, my grandmother says, there is a cocaine bust every day. She hears it all happening on her police scanner that she keeps turned on all day in her kitchen.

 I track the last scrap of his black bear back between the branches.

 –Coming or what?

This forest is a dry box I could sit down in, gather the walls around me, make a hood from the soft brown leaves and all the needles like matches and eyelashes. I will forget about the wet black rainforest we were in an hour ago. I'll build a fort and roast pine cones and eat the sweet feet of mice trapped inside that I've heard about in campfire stories all my life, before they cut down every last tree, every last piece of this place, like he says they will. This whole island will be a bare rock in the ocean off Vancouver. The ferries will charge tourists to come here and climb up its dry sides, read plaques bolted to the rocks about living things that used to be here, look at satellite photos of rainforest canopies, black skies stencilled with life, the faces of the countries of men that immigrated to slice them down, our coast written into the context of the dinosaurs, all the old, dead things made magic by doom. That's what he says.

– How come you brought your machete this time if you don't need it here.

We walk quickly over the dry, crackling ground. Instead of sweating, sharp ferns there's a deep carpet of rotting branches and salal.

– Machete's not only for bush. No other humanoids out here you're gonna see. Lots that could happen.

He stops, puts up one hand, turns to face me.

– You hear that?

I stop.

I hear wind like decks of cards being shuffled by invisible players crouching in the bushes and, under everything, a hum. One bird. Two birds. Four?

– I don't hear anything.

– Yeah you do. You hear the forest. And you think the forest gives a shit about you?

He doesn't say it like a challenge, just like it's true.

– No. Yeah. Yeah, maybe it does. Yeah, it does. No. Does it?

– Yeah it does.

– So. Then why'd you bring the machete then?

–Makes me feel more safe.

–Carrying a knife would make me feel more scared.

–That's cause you don't know how to use a knife.

–So show me then.

So he does. The handle heavy in my hand. The blade shows my whole face, my chin sliced off at the light-slicked edge, my eyes sliding away. My arm sinks under its weight when I don't concentrate on it, supporting its heavy threat.

–You gotta move it fast and know where you're aiming. Never cut toward yourself. Always aim away. You could cut your leg off like that, little girl. Wouldn't be the only leg here, though.

He promises me a graveyard.

He's the one who teaches me these things, every time my parents drive up here. How to stop a boy from breathing with my two thumbs, their joints glued together like a wishbone's V. How to skin and whittle a branch so it flies and breaks skin. How to build a fire on a beach. Find the dry wood between the big beach logs. The ocean spits up those logs like toothpicks. Your body is floss.

Back in Vancouver, I keep these lessons for myself. The cherry blossom trees that foam up pink around the school hold secret weapons.

Everybody in my city family looks down on him — his grammar, his gym shorts worn to dinner, his swearing, the pattern of his sweat around his T-shirt collar like a tattoo.

–What'd you mean asking me is my mom crazy?

I'm surprised how angry I sound, but if I take it back, he won't answer.

–She's not all there.

He keeps walking, shrugs, like it's just obvious.

My legs hurt but I won't say so. He swings his camera now instead of his knife. The lens cap hangs loose and the camera's glass eye flashes like a pool of black oil at his hip. It's late afternoon, light coming down thicker through the branches, stamping the ground with spines and teeth, as if skeletons are slung in the canopy, throwing down sharp shadows, and we are wandering the open spaces between their bones.

–Loggers'll trash the town when they get to it. Clearcutting'll get there this summer. They cut down more every summer. Want to get some good shots for the album.

He has a closet full of photos of the trips he's gone on around this part of the island since he was a teenager.

–What do you mean my mom's not all there?

He stops and takes the ghost town book out of his bag, stands in the shadow of a huge tree and flips through the pages.

–Yup, we're almost there.

His baseball cap is pulled low over his eyes, his shoulders thick and blocky as chunks of fireplace rock.

–Just tell me.

I know he's the only one who'll tell me the truth. Everyone else lies to my face about my mom. I know it. They say it's stress. She's under a lot of stress right now. Or, work takes a lot out of her. Or, she needs more time for herself. I know that they are all lying. Other people's anger isn't like hers, and I know it. I know that one day she will get angry and she will be gone. I spend a lot of time imagining it happening in different ways.

She'll explode, a red cartoon bomb. She'll fade piece by piece like the people in *Back to the Future*, sucked away, cheeks then feet then hair, clutching her chest for air. She'll breathe me in. Or nothing will happen. She'll just disappear.

– Not all there. Not all there.

He looks down at me.

– She don't look me in the eye. Ever seen her get really mad? She don't know how to stop. I don't know, kid. Not all there. Means something's missing. Don't know what. Just not there.

I look at him, my voice floating away from my body.

– Was it there before?

The forest's dark fills in all the lines in his face. I can't tell what he's thinking. I can never tell what he's thinking. He shrugs, shadows like green pillows on his shoulders.

– Don't matter, does it. Now that it's gone, eh?


He carries me on his back when I can't walk anymore. Hook my arms around him, float on his body.

– You can sleep if you want.

– But then I'd let go and fall.

His Adam's apple buzzes under my linked fingers like a drowsy bee cupped there.

– If you fall asleep hanging on really tight, your hands'll stay that way. Gotta hold on tight.


He rocks me a bit.

– Here we are little girl. Here's your ghost town.

I pull my tired eyes open and see lines in the night between his neck and shoulder.

–Look this was the road they made through it.

His flashlight's on, snagging on roots, leaves jumping out like wallpaper rockets, and the yellow tube of light wanders slow over grassy spaces between the walls of trees, like one eye we're both seeing through.

–You seeing it? You awake?

He walks faster down the middle of the road. He breathes fast, excited.

The flashlight chooses for us. The front of a white church worked over by bugs, tides of dried needles and leaves lining the old road as if the ocean washed them here, a door standing without its walls, darkness surrounding both sides completely, the carcass of some animal at its stoop, struck dead trying to go through that door to what was on the other side.

–Holy shit lookit that.

I don't, whatever it is he's found now. I hide from the ghost town behind his neck. I feel the shapes of the dead houses around us as we walk slowly down the main street.

He puts me down on an ancient tree's arched root, tall as a bench, and we drink Mountain Dew and chew pepperoni and white bread. He puts an arm around me and pulls me against him until I stop shaking, shivering.

Tomorrow I will drive back to the city with my parents. The ferry ride to the mainland will feel, like it always does, like a crossing between worlds. My mom will cry in the ferry line-up, scream at the apologetic BC Ferries guy in his navy shirt, her voice rising like shrill wind. I will want her to disappear, beg for her to disappear.

–Pretty neat, eh? Glad we came. Too dark for photos though.

He'll come back here, again and again, until the logging company carves its own road through this forest. Then he'll come and take photos of the clear-cut when they're finished, the small white stumps he always says look like grave markers.

–Good you saw this girl. It'll all be gone, soon enough.

# LIKE
# MIND

**SO WILLIAM** was away from Vancouver for a few years. I heard scraps of news about him from friends but no one wanted to say much. It was as if he'd died and we didn't want to take his name in vain or anger a ghost. He was somewhere removed from us, Victoria or Edmonton or a private university in a small town, studying art or working a secretarial job for the government or something else. I asked Quinn, our mutual friend, where William had ended up and he said, "I think somewhere

it snows a lot. He mentioned it was snowing in an email." He
never sent me any news of weather, just blank emails with
MP3s attached.

So I was older when he came back. I was living forty minutes
by bus outside of Vancouver. A block from the ocean. When I
moved in I didn't know Tova's house was on the bird migration
route. One morning I woke up and heard a fleet of fighter jets
outside. Looked out the window and the sky was solid black, a
winged swarm, and sudden, complete silence when the thousands of birds landed in the water a block away.

This stuff he got off that Internet list. I couldn't believe it when
he called me up, his voice precisely the same as before.

–Hey I'm back in town and need help moving stuff into my
new place.

–You're back in Vancouver?

–Yeah.

–What for how long?

–Don't know. Needed to get out of E-town. Shithole. You
still with Tova? She's got a car right?

He called Edmonton E-town; that's where he was from.

–What do you need to move?

His voice curved. Evasive, sing-songy.

–Just a bunch of different stuff. Nothing major.

–What, from friends' places? Or Craigslist?

–No no. This other thing. Everything's free. All this shit people want to get rid of. You gotta pick it up yourself, otherwise

it's completely free. Anyway I set up a bunch of pickups for Friday. You're the only person I know who has a car.

–It's Tova's car.

–It'll just be a couple hours. I'll buy you lunch.

–I think I'm working.

–Quinn told me you're free Thursdays and Fridays. Please please please Laura.

After I wrote down his address, an apartment in Yaletown he was sharing with three international students, I vacuumed our whole condo. One furious push. One phone call was all it took, I sucked every corner clean of dust, after all that time, I stripped gray fur from the bright white baseboards, I threw the dog bed onto the deck and scalded every dish in the sink. I called Quinn.

–William's back in town. I'm helping him move on Friday, apparently. He's getting everything off some Internet thing for free stuff?

Quinn knew all about it. He'd pulled his shit together, was pretty stable, had even had lunch with him already, there'd been an unrequited boy in Edmonton who liked concerts and Amaretto. William had called everyone we knew in Vancouver before he'd called me.


November sunshine, scorch of cold. He appeared from the black mirrored doors of his building in flip-flops and a white knit hat, swivelled, spotted me, waved high above his head, like he was flagging down a plane.

–Thank you so much for coming. Thank you so so much.

–Hi.

He was still using the same cologne. Scent threw me back. As if we had been lovers before. How much weight he'd gained, about twenty pounds, but still all careful swift movements, his face a toy weather system.

Body slam hug, his friendly smothering.

– Thanks so much.

– No worries.

Autopilot's dead skin around my voice.

– The first place's in Burnaby. Kingsway. Past all the pho places.

– God, that's far.

– Sorry. But it's for a desk! That's the first thing.

– Are you taking classes?

– No.

– What're doing?

Yaletown passed us by, the turn onto Main street, up past the new condos and backpacker places, past the 24/7 McDonalds, Broadway up there swarming.

He was just hanging around, trying to find work, paying not much for his room, but there wasn't any work around really, recession and all the arts cuts.

– Well what kind of work are you looking for William?

– Something easy, you know, that doesn't require me to think publicly.

– How many places are we picking stuff up from?

– Not too many. The desk is first.

– Put on the radio if you want.

Truncated song bursts, announcers' downbeats, half a sentence from an ad for life insurance, who believes radio ads for life insurance? Bonnie Raitt singing I can't make you, love me.

I made him stay with CBC for five minutes for the traffic report, the weather, and then he left it on the university's student station, a DJ with bottle-opener breath hits on the mic. A song we'd danced to in undergrad.

His fingers making shadow puppets in fall sunlight on the dash. Traffic organized by the music's erratic rhythm. Ten minutes of stoplight idling.

The first pickup was easy. The IKEA desk had been disassembled and left leaning in a brick entranceway in the upscale condo development. The owner had left a baggie containing screws and an Allen key taped to the desk. I took one end of the desk's surface and William took the other and we slid the desk into Tova's car, local kids staring from their bikes.

–Are you stealing that, I'm gonna call the police.

The kid bounced his bike side to side, HARRISON in black permanent marker across the handlebars.

–You are the police Harrison. We are the police, William said.

The kid stared hard almost tears or hurt blindness, then sped away toward a woman on the corner. A column, a caretaker.

The woman slapped her hands around the kid's handlebars, glared at us, teenagers or thieves.

We drove away laughing.

Tova is my lover and she is a reasonable person. She said, You want to borrow my car to do what? You're helping who move? He phones you out of the blue and you just say yes?

Water under the bridge. Got to move on sometime. Everyone

deserves a second chance. So I said, I don't have a good reason, okay? I just need to borrow your car.

She left the room without speaking. Left me to the pour of this. This is yours this is not mine.


He was happy with the desk. Birch veneer, silver handles, concealed hinges. He kept looking at it over his shoulder.

He read out an address in East Van, near Broadway and Nanaimo. Rain tore at the windshield. Tova's stuffed elephants swung from the rear-view. I eyed them self-consciously.

I tried to see how many addresses he'd written on the piece of paper he incessantly checked. Just a couple hours, he kept telling me, though an hour had already passed. Thank you so much, he kept saying. Thank you so so much for helping me.

–So what were you up to in Edmonton?

–Not too much. Hung out with people. From high school mostly.

–How was that?

–Good. It was good to be around people who don't know I'm a fucking nutbar.

His expression in the rearview wasn't baiting or hurt. He watched the road. East Broadway. It was just statement of fact.

–I guess that would be a good break.

–Yeah. Think I needed just, a break from everything.

–Where were you living?

–With my mom. You know I wasn't allowed to live on my own, right?

–How'd it go?

–She needed some company. I hadn't been back since the divorce. I helped her calm down a bit.

–Calm down?

–She smoked pot with me.

I pictured them in the conservative living room where William had grown up. Inside the house William had told me about years ago, inside the city he'd left furiously, flamboyantly when he was eighteen, three years before I'd met him. Inside a thick cloud their bodies drift side by side, his long and bending hands always flailing gesturing fingers always whispering punctuation, her body squat and compacted sitting solidly beside her son, doing his drugs with him, and him breathing in the smoke and breathing it out, breathing depression in and breathing it out, and her doing it with him, how else can she take care of her son who needs pills to be sane and needs to vanish into clouds to survive?

–I think this is it. What's the address again?

–Yeah this it. Beanbag chair!

He left me in the car to sit with the things I'd planned to say, furiously. Now a childish murmuring, overdone lyrics, an embarrassing poem from when I was thirteen years old and in love with my own reflection. I used to stare at myself, change my face, stare, smile, test. Ratio of tooth to lip. Chin slant. Breath intake, cheek swell, how should I lose this skin today?

The rain beat on the car's tin shell.

What the fuck William? What are you doing now?

Because there he was, again. Slaloming across the lawn, deep in tall streaks of rain, bending, losing his centre of gravity, arms straight out around a circle of red. The beanbag chair, vinyl, coated in rain, bright as a life raft.

The beanbag chair sliding into the back seat, back door slamming, passenger door opening, his sudden hot breathing anxiety.

–Drive drive drive.

–What?

Another figure coming across the lawn. A woman, tall, holding a shoe in each hand, slapping air with the shoes, and her mouth open.

–William.

–Drive.

I drove. We swerved into the centre of the quiet street, a tree-lined street, two dark green tree-lines the edges of my vision. A corner, another street. Then we were on Nanaimo. Dim sum, all day breakfast, houses.

I pulled over.

–What the fuck was that?

–She said she didn't put it online. Her boyfriend did. But it was hers.

–So you took it.

–He said I could. In his email. I need it for the corner.

–The corner?

–Of my room. Look, I drew a plan.

He pulled a neatly folded sheet of paper from his pocket. A small, orderly map. Bed and a round object labelled TABLE FOR READING in one corner; BEANBAG CHAIR in another corner; BOOKCASE in one corner, the books sketched in faintly; DESK in the fourth corner; and FLAT-SCREEN TV; VCR; and

BUDDHA LAMP; and MICROWAVE; SMALL SPACE HEATER; and TUNNEL. I looked away.

–Tunnel?

–Someone's giving one away. Like a kid's play tunnel.

–Why do you want that?

–I want to get a cat.

–William.

–What?

–You can't have a cat. Can you?

He folded the room plan and slid it back into his pocket. Pulled his white knit hat down over his curly hair. He took the list out of his pocket and watched it in the pale light. The downpour had vanished upward, leaving gleaming sky like new skin.

–But I have roommates.

–Sorry.

–The cat would be fine.

–Okay. Sorry. Sorry.

–You know. I'm not like I was. I'm on my own again now.

–Yeah I know.

–I'm back in Vancouver.

–I know.

–No one wants to talk to me.

–They will.

–Vancouver is a city of owls.

I looked at my watch.

–William, they just don't know what to say to you. What are they supposed to say to you?

–Hello? I hate people who hide. Do they think it was my fucking fault?

He leaned forward, twisted his fingers behind his neck. The afternoon light through the car windows siphoning into his mind. He was always too sensitive. No filters. That was how I had explained it to Tova, when I'd begun to explain what had happened to William. No filters. People need filters. He wound, unwound his fingers, fingertips digging into the back of his neck. I knew how to wait for him to surface again. I turned on the radio, at first quietly, then louder after a few minutes. Bonnie Raitt was singing again. Her voice, flooding, trembling.

–How long have I been gone anyway? Not that long. Couple years.

–Almost three years. You had lunch with Quinn right? I talked to him.

–Quinn's nice to everyone. Even Kyle won't talk to me. Only a bit. He said he had to go but it was obvious he didn't. There was a TV in the background and people. Probably a party he didn't invite me to.

–Did you tell him you were coming back?

–We lived together for two and a half years.

I looked at the drawing of his room again.

–Someone's really giving away a flat-screen TV?

–Yeah. You wouldn't believe all the stuff people put on this list.

The pickup place for the flat screen was in North Van so I took a right and then we headed north down Boundary. Toward the Second Narrows bridge, the mountains at eye level.

Printed blue in a ring around my mind since childhood: is everyone who grew up in Vancouver incapable of imagining a city not dwarfed by its sheltering, indifferent mountains?

Today the mountains are dressed in white sun, volcanic with cloud.

Crossing the bridge:

–What does Tova do?

–She's a nurse.

–What kind?

–She works in the spinal unit at VGH.

–Jesus. She must see a lot of shit.

–Yeah. You know when the most spinal injuries happen? Around Christmas, because everyone's up in the mountains. Snowboarding. You know how many teenaged boys get paralyzed snowboarding?

–Doesn't it drive her nuts?

–No, she's solid.

–How long've you been together?

–A little over three years.

–I never met her.

–You and me weren't talking much then.

–You didn't want to introduce her to me. You didn't want her to meet me.

–What makes you think I even told her about you?

His laughter hit the windshield, launched from his polished teeth.

–What's so funny.

–That's such bullshit. She probably didn't want to lend you her car to do this.

–No, she didn't.

–She thinks you shouldn't be talking to me. She thinks I'm bad for you. That you'll come home upset all over again.

–Stop it, William.

–Thanks for helping me anyway.

–I'm only helping you because no one else would. That's the only reason.


The last time I saw him before he left Vancouver was at a party at Quinn's apartment, after his third or fourth hospital stay. In the building at Main and Broadway with the elevator shaft sticking out of the roof like a too-small hat. Quinn's apartment — walls decorated with his collection of vintage clocks, narrow bookcases full of CDs. Quinn had been my friend before I'd met William; when William and I met, Quinn and I adopted him, took him to concerts, to our favourite restaurants and cafes. He had the constant smiling of a person who needed to be shown what to do next. Conversation was his compulsion, a sparkling net he used to wrap himself up.

At that party, all the people who knew William circled him warily. He had become a reputation. I lost track of him and ended up in the closet-sized kitchen with Quinn. We talked about William; we couldn't talk without talking about William, what happened to William, what is going on with William, what's the latest with William?

–Stop worrying about it so much Laura. He's going to do what he's going to do.

–You've been watching him this whole time too.

–You can't watch him all the time.

I heard Quinn sigh and open the fridge as I left the kitchen.

I found William in a corner of the living room. His boyfriend Kyle a few feet away, glancing constantly, nervously. William was demonstrating how to solve a Rubik's cube for a girl I didn't know. I stood and watched.

William's thin hands rotated, the colours morphing between his palms. William's thin, pale hands. His fingers flickered, a changing shelter for the inside thing. The sections of colour slipped and shifted, the girl watching. Laughing uncontrollably, she put a hand over her mouth and William smiled, watching the Rubik's cube. He'd memorized the procedure when he was in high school to impress a boy — I knew the whole story, had heard it many times. He loved to tell the same stories over and over, the way other people like to put their favourite song on repeat. I listened for which details remained the same, which details changed.

The girl was still laughing, William still smiling, when Kyle stepped forward and took the Rubik's cube from William's hand.

–Kyle!

–Stop it.

–What?

–It's stupid, just stop it.

Kyle turned from shouting at William to shout at the girl.

–He's done this a million times, okay? A million times. So don't be impressed. He does this for everybody. Haven't you ever seen a Rubik's cube before?

The girl stared at William, at his empty hand.

Quinn rushed out of the gathering crowd. Put his arm on Kyle's shoulder.

–Kyle.

–What are you doing?

–Kyle. It doesn't matter, Quinn said.

Kyle put one hand over his face and let Quinn take the Rubik's cube. Quinn handed the Rubik's cube back to William.

–You can do the rest of the trick now.

But the girl who had been watching and smiling drifted into the crowd, holding her wine stiffly. William put the Rubik's cube in his jacket pocket.

–Why can't you just let me be normal?

–I didn't do this to you.

–I didn't make this happen I didn't make this happen.

I can't remember anymore who left the party first, William or Kyle. William called me the next day and apologized over and over for ruining the party. He told me, as he always did before hanging up, that he loved me. I heard that Kyle asked him to move out and thought, how could he, and I also thought, good for him, he's sacrificed enough of himself already. After that, William screened my calls. He was spiralling again. I knew, from the texture of the silence, that his resistance was quietly falling, again. Not long after, I heard he'd left Vancouver.


He read out the North Van address for the flat-screen TV.

Someone else, he said, was giving away a VCR and a box of videotapes.

–Old videotapes?

–Yeah. They said I could tape over the stuff, but they want to get rid of them at the same time as the VCR.

–Wonder what's on the tapes.

–How big's the trunk?

–Probably have to put the TV in the back seat with the desk.

–Hope we don't run out of space.

–I didn't know we'd be hauling everything but the kitchen sink.

–Thanks again for helping me, Laura. You have no idea how much this helps me.

Did he say thank you that often before? I couldn't remember.

–It's okay. I should call Tova soon, though. Tell her we still have a few things to get. She worries.

–Is she off work soon?

–She was having lunch with a friend. Then she's on the evening shift.

–She gets off late?

–Yeah, I need to pick her up later. After we're done.

He looked at me anxiously, waiting for the invitation to meet Tova. I could not put Tova and William in the same car.

Her mannered fury. *Do you know what you put her through?*

–I think this is the place.

The house was set high above the street, its address in woodcuts on a large rock beside the sidewalk at the foot of a steep flight of stone steps. I looked up. Sheer glass sides; balconies outlined with rain-worn cedar. Downhill landscaping in stages of falling water. Strong coastal plants grasping earth.

The view they must have of the ocean from up there. Out over the small bank of city, over the low-lying ocean, Stanley Park a black-green finger nudging just the edge of the eye.

–Beautiful.

–Rich people.

We climbed the steps to the house. William was breathless by the time we got to the top.

–You're out of shape.

–That's what happens when you spend your life smoking dope in your mom's basement.

I laughed.

–My life's a fucking mess.

–Whatever. Lots of people I know can't find work. I'm only working part-time.

–You have Tova.

No one came to the door when he rang the doorbell.

–Did they say you should call first?

–No, the guy just said to knock.

I could tell the front door was handmade. Cedar, carved with concentric circles that swirled at the bottom, leaving the frame of the door. The design continued in the set of the slate on the top step; shards of slate wandered into the garden before dispersing under bushes. William pointed at the wandering slate.

–An artist lives here.

Footsteps rang out inside the house, wandered and faded like soft drumbeats, and the door opened.

–Yes? Can I help you?

–I'm here. We're here. You put a TV on the Internet?

The man ran his fingers along the inside edge of the door.

–Right. You're William. It's in the back room.

We followed him through an entranceway built like an atrium. A large stone bowl rested in the centre of the floor, as if to collect rainwater.

We passed next through a dining room. Long cedar table: one half of a split trunk. Oiled, the rings in the grain shining. One wall held two prints in balance, ovals of red and black, outline of one wing vanishing. Each print the inverse of the other. The cedar table screamed its pure red light. *Wow*, William mouthed at me. I nodded, rushed forward, suddenly ashamed to be walked through this space to pick up a rejected TV.

Then the living room. A toddler's oversized plastic toys heaped in front of the fireplace. A woman's jacket thrown across the back of a couch, still thick with perfume. By the fireplace, a cardboard boxful of picture frames. William pointed to the box. A large photo tilted into it, showing two figures. An ocean view. *Divorce!* he mouthed. I shook my head. My eyes tilted. *Don't.*

The man walked slowly ahead of us. He was wearing suede loafers, chocolate-brown corduroys, an open-collared white shirt and a tan sweater that hung loosely, clung slightly. We followed him down a short hall. The light followed him.

Into his study. The flat-screen TV leaned against a bookcase. Beside it sat the VCR and a large cardboard box of videotapes. Each tape had been carefully labeled.

–There it is. It's yours. You can find your own way out.

Something muttered, whispered.

His leaving muttered, feet slipping into the dim hallway.

Have a good day or Good-day or Good-bye.

Find your own way out Good-bye Please Good-bye Day Please.

–And then he left his house and walked directly into the ocean.

–Don't be an asshole, William.

–I was kidding.

–Let's just get the stuff and get out of here.

–The TV looks like it's in great shape.

–I feel like a carrion bird. You take the TV, your arms are longer.

I set the VCR on top of the videotapes and picked up the box.

I tried not to look at the labels. JUSTIN'S 1ST BIRTHDAY.

  –I saw a wedding guestbook on the list once.

  –I don't want to know.


We walked quickly through the hall, through the living room, through the dining room, past the felled tree polished for humans to eat off, past the dark divided sky of the art on the wall. Somewhere distantly I heard footsteps. The atrium. Those windows large as walls. A person could swim through the glass and find himself underwater, his back a reflection of a sinking mountain. We left the house.


We drove silently to the Starbucks five minutes away on Lonsdale Avenue. The man's loneliness in my chest, a crouched siren.

  –Get me a grande latte and a chickpea wrap? Get yourself something, whatever.

  I gave him twenty bucks and he sprang from the car.

  Tova answered her cell on the seventh ring.

  –Hey. I'm working.

  –I'm with him.

  –How's it going? Has he lit anyone on fire yet?

  –I wish I hadn't said I'd help him with this.

  Her breath heavy and slow on the other end of the line.

  –Yeah, I thought that might happen. Can you stop?

  –No. No one will help him. He said no one will even talk to him.

  –Can you blame them?

–Why am I the one stuck with him?

–Because you still feel responsible for him?

–What? I haven't fucking even talked to him for three years.

–I'm at work. I gotta go, sweetie.

–We went to this guy's house and got a flat-screen TV. Huge, fancy TV. Sony. Really expensive. But we had to take this box of old VHS tapes with it. They were obviously, like, tapes of his whole family. That's why he was giving away the flat screen, you know? To get rid of the tapes, to get someone else to take the tapes away. He was the saddest person I've ever seen. William was making jokes the whole time and I was thinking, God, this is what makes you crazy, you know, you can just, not notice this, and then, we just left. The tapes are in the back seat.

Rhythmic white noise of the hospital in the background. Voice pressing urgency through the speaker system; a heavy door clattering shut.

–Where is he now?

–In Starbucks. I sent him for lattes.

–Drive away. Just drive away.

–Just leave him here?

–Just do it. Just drive. I have to go, sweetie. I'll call you when my shift ends. I'm sorry. You're picking me up after my shift right?

–Yeah.

Through the large front window of the Starbucks I could see him waiting for the lattes at the counter. The barista a solemn mechanic behind the two silver coffee machines. William moved side to side, a child's impatient small wanders.

Tova is a reasonable person. When first I told her the story of what had happened to William she said, "Did you ever think that you were just in over your head?"

"No," I said. Tova and I had been dating for a few months. She looked worried.

"Not even a little?"

I wondered if she was making fun of me.

"No. I didn't even think about it."

A year after I met her, I moved into her condo a half hour bus ride south of Vancouver. She'd bought the condo when she got her job at the hospital. Investment's practiced foothold. The small distance from Vancouver brought me a relief I didn't expect. Two bridges and a road. The shore, a protected area for migratory birds, a block away. We were on a walk at night the second time I saw them. There was no difference between the solid layer of wings and the sky. Or it was the sky, splitting and scattering. There was no difference between the sound and the feeling of the sound, a cascading darkness dividing around us. Soft wings splitting, the impression of bodies carving a space, a generous loud space. I closed my eyes and stopped walking. Could I hear one wing? The sound of the birds continued, continued. Thickness. How many? Just thickness, enough to fill. The wandering screaming of their speech. They came out of all the holes in the sky like their own kind of weather.

There is screaming from inside the Starbucks.

–What are you doing?

–What? What?

–Are you nuts?

–He just threw it all over me. Just threw it.

–Do you know him? Who knows him? Is there anyone here that knows him?

–I know him.

A man and a woman turned and stared at me. Both in their forties. Dressed well. North Vancouver people, professionals. William stood behind them, pale, holding the two cups. I only saw that he was shaking, his head down, and I made myself look away.

Latte in a spreading milky pool on the slate floor. Bright black boots on slate floor, surrounding by the latte. A child's bright rubber boots in a puddle, stomping.

–You know him? Are you with him?

–What happened?

Latte down the front of the woman's leather jacket. Her forehead clenched by a waxed hairstyle. I saw her rings, the weighted cold silver of her watch. The man stepped forward. He raised his hands to speak. His cufflinks spoke. A pure silver voice.

–This young man attacked my wife.

Who said "young man" anymore?

–What happened. I was in my car.

–I was standing here speaking with my husband and I asked him to move please so I could get our drinks from the counter and he yelled at me and refused to move and then he threw his boiling drink all over me. I'm lucky I wasn't burned. But my jacket is ruined. And it's leather. The leather is ruined.

–Someone will have to pay for it.

–Someone is going to pay for the jacket.

–William?

–Is he okay? How do you know him? Are you his . . . Are you paid to go around with him?

–William?

–What's his last name?

The man took a step toward William. William stepped back. He leaned into a wire stand displaying rows of shining red bags of West Coast Blend. William looked at me carefully. He shook his head and put out his hands.

–William?

–William. William. This lady is here to help you.

–Stop it.

–Who is going to pay for my jacket?

The barista drifted from behind the counter. Oversized green Starbucks apron, pixie haircut.

The woman pointed at the barista.

–You saw. You saw what happened.

–Tell her what happened.

The barista stared at the woman, looked terrified for a moment, turned her head, thinking.

–I didn't see all of it.

–You saw most of it. You were behind the counter.

–Okay, okay. The guy was waiting for his lattes and they were late. He kept saying he was worried someone called Laura was going to drive away and leave him here. So he was telling us to hurry up. He kept apologizing, over and over, it was really weird. He was talking really fast.

–Yes. That was when he threw the lattes all over my jacket.

–No, you were telling him to hurry up. He shook his elbow.

–I hardly touched him.

–He seemed really scared.

–Of someone touching his elbow? That's ridiculous.

The barista turned to me.

–Look, you know him, right? Can you just get out of here. If there's a fight in here we're supposed to call the manager. He lives in Surrey though. Do you need help? My brother's autistic.

–He isn't autistic.

–Someone has to pay for my jacket. Are you his social worker? Can you tell me his last name? Who are you?

The barista stared at me uncertainly.

–If you want to take him to a hospital you have to prove you're related, right?

At the word *hospital* William stepped forward.

–Are you related to him?

–He's my brother.

–He's your brother. What's your last name? I'm going to file a report.

–I'm taking him to the hospital. I'm sorry about your jacket. William. William. We're leaving. William.

I grabbed his elbow. As we rushed out the door I heard the man shout at the barista, Who is going to pay for the jacket! The jacket is ruined! Starbucks is going to pay for the jacket!

The street was solid with traffic. I bludgeoned the crosswalk button with my palm until the light shone green. Cars screamed up and down the street. I held onto his elbow, across the street, the cars screaming, wheels and I could hear seagulls from Lonsdale Quay two blocks away, and I opened the passenger door for him and helped him inside and went to my side and the door clicked open and then shut behind me.

He put his head between his knees and breathed deeply. He'd been taught how to breathe, to soothe himself. I remembered that he'd had to take courses in self-soothing when he was in the hospital. All the times I'd visited him in the hospital the people at the other white tables in the visiting room had stared numbly into space and I'd wondered why these people needed lessons in self-soothing, they seemed like vegetables. But they must all have had the time when they had broken, their time of vanishing, and who had been there to watch that? I exchanged smiles with other visitors in the hallways. The regretful smiles of survivors.

He breathed. The breath of hunger, of growling, and then softer as the panic left his body. He let the air sing through his throat. He used his stomach.

–I'm not taking you to the hospital. I just said that to get us out of there.

–I know.

–Oh fuck. Get down.

We pressed our chests into our laps, waited while the couple came out of the Starbucks, their faces bent with frustration, and walked off down Lonsdale Avenue toward the ocean. William turned his head. One vein shaking in his forehead. Old ache in my running shoes.

–I'm sorry Laura. It happened just, so fast.

–I know.

–It's not supposed to happen anymore.

The couple would be gone by now.

We stayed bent over, below the noise of the street.

–How long's it been?

–Few months.

–Who was there?

–I was on the bus.

–What happened?

–Police.

–Jesus.

–My mom came and got me. She's used to it.

–She was okay with you leaving Edmonton?

He rocked his feet back and forth.

–I didn't tell her I was leaving.

–William.

–I couldn't do it to her anymore. I mean, I'm twenty-*nine*. I'm going to be *thirty*.

–But she was okay with you being there, right?

–That isn't the point.

–William. Does she know you're in Vancouver?

–Kyle called her. She reported me missing.

–She must have been crazy worried, William. How could you do that to her?

–I just got on a bus.

–Have you seen Kyle?

–He won't see me. He said he's with someone else now.

–Who?

–He wouldn't tell me his name. He said he couldn't know me anymore. That he didn't want to hear from me at all. He hung up on me.

I waited while he cried into his netted hands. Tears jelled between his fingers.

No one knew what Kyle saw. During the year before William's first hospital stay I had thought their relationship was normal. Together at parties they were whimsical, charmed by each other's punch lines — a lightweight silver hinge. An easy couple to invite. When they'd met I'd thought Kyle was perfect for William's distracted energy, his impulsive need for response. William would regularly send me thirty emails in a row — one long sentence written in thirty different ways — and I'd thought that was normal, an intelligent pattern seen by like minds. Kyle was slower and better.

I asked Kyle once. When did you know? He shrugged. Know? He got angry. He never got angry. Know what? Know what? People get depressed. People do stuff because they're depressed. Does that mean they're crazy? Does that mean they're crazy?

They lived together for more than two years in a small apartment off Main, in the neighbourhood full of students who knitted in cafes. I hung out with William often in their apartment. Kyle arrived home from his job, showed me how his mother made chow mein; William kept a folder of images he clipped out of the newspaper tucked on top of the fridge so that he wouldn't misplace it; their balcony was precisely the width of two metal fold-up picnic chairs sitting side-by-side; they used one of their kitchen cupboards to store photo albums; birds nested inside the roof of their building; the scratch of their singing, the chopped whisper and beat of wings between the ceiling and the roof; these are the things I remember; every relationship is its own secret.

I sat up and late afternoon sunlight pierced the windshield. Brightness knocked my eyes backward. Blinking, breaking and filtering light. William sat up. He could breathe now.

–What's the next thing on the list?

–Let's stop. You don't have to. Let's just stop.

The map of his room was sticking out of his pocket. I reached out and took it.

–Microwave. Space heater. Buddha lamp. Chair. Tunnel.

–No tunnel. Remember? No cat.

–No cat.

–Microwave. Space heater. Buddha lamp?

–It's a lamp, shaped like a Buddha. It was the only lamp I could find. I checked for days. I need a lamp to read.

–Are you completely broke?

–I've got some money, not much. I was working the government secretary job my dad got me. I just want a schedule. Time sucks when you've got a lot of it.

–Did you apply to, like, Starbucks?

–Laura. Once they look me up, they know I've been crazy. It's like having a criminal record. You don't pass go.

–Doesn't that just mean they have a probation period or whatever?

–Crazy-record means no job. Trust me. It's worse than being a criminal.

–Could your dad get you another job, here?

–He's pissed that I left. They want me to stay in my mom's basement in Edmonton for the rest of my life.

–You're not supposed to be living on your own?

–I did everything. All the counseling, all the tests. All the everything. I finished it. I can do whatever the hell I want now.

We drove across the Lion's Gate bridge back to Vancouver. I remembered how small the bridge had looked from the man's house where we'd picked up the flat screen. A frail line drawn across the water by a human hand.

After the bridge, we turned and drove the curving road through Stanley Park. Along the edge where the windstorm tore down the forest a few years before, around the time he left Vancouver. It took months for the city to clear away the wreckage. *The Vancouver Sun* ran photos of split trees lying across the jogging path on the seawall. The exposed stunningly white and red flesh of trees. In less than a day, the wind had dragged the forest out of itself, had hurled the remains against the rock and water.

The road curved back through the park, away from the ocean.

Out of the park and into the West End.

–Still want coffee? I could use one.

–Yeah. Sure.

I parked on a side street and he hurried to the Blenz on Denman. What if the car hadn't been within sight of the Starbucks? That couple would have called the police. He would have been in the same place in another city.

I texted Tova: *He had a panic attack.*

I texted Quinn: *He went nuts in a Starbucks. You should have done this with me.*

I'd barely flipped my phone shut when it chimed.

Quinn's text: *He showed me that room drawing when we had lunch. Haha.*

I flipped the phone open and shut, its screen winking at me, open shut. Open. Shut. Blue-white. Silent. Tova was still on her shift.

Quinn's apartment was a few blocks away. He lived downtown with two roommates. Their tiny two-level apartment smelled of their sweat, of breakfast frittata, of pot, of the quilt balled on the couch in front of the flat-screen TV that doubled as their computer monitor. Quinn had passed into his late twenties without changing. Sometimes I thought his optimism buoyed him; sometimes I thought it was his indifference. Tova, he'd told me, was turgid. But I love her, I'd said, and he'd shrugged; I'm just being honest. He stopped introducing me to the men he dated. The first time William was in the hospital, Quinn and I had gone together to visit him. We were children playing an adult game. William apologized. He hadn't wanted anyone to be hurt, he said. He wanted to just be gone and everyone would forget. Quinn lowered his head and said, I'm sorry I wasn't there anymore. William said, I'm sorry you guys should just go I'm sorry I dragged you into this. We stayed for an hour and afterward sat in the hallway outside the ward until a nurse glared at us and told us there was a waiting room for visitors. We left the hospital and walked down to Broadway and then all the way down Broadway to Burrard, down Burrard and across the bridge to the seawall and English Bay.

We walked for hours.

Quinn said, I had no idea, I knew he wasn't doing well but I didn't know, I didn't know it was this, it was this bad. I said, I knew, I was the only one who knew, even Kyle didn't know, but I knew, and I didn't do anything to stop it. You couldn't have stopped it, it's just an illness, like a virus, like any other illness, it's just in the body. Illness is illness is illness. No it was there always. In his stuttering smiles, his run-on sentences and run-on thoughts, polished curves of his thoughts and seeping uncertainties, the cold space of choking overwhelming memory, he never forgot anything, and how people who met him said he had a chip missing or he was always too much, too intense at parties and too many questions for the bus driver, every small thing became a symptom and a sign, a beckoning, is that where it is, it was always there in the way his head hung like a bathysphere waiting for the bus in a rainstorm and he turned and drank the water in like sparks, it had always been there, arguing with pathologies is useless is harmless is everything when eccentricity slides to sickness, but there it was again, him hiding in the bathroom at a concert a few months before the first breakdown because the drums were shouting at him, but he always spoke in metaphors, in whimsies, and no he wasn't obsessive he was a hoarder of sentiments, he did not have paranoid delusion he held his hand up beside the transparency of a rained-on leaf and saw two leaves, and that is it, there, there, a sliver or a shade, it can be tracked back to the first conversation and held onto, shown, not a slide or a vanishing.


–Laura? Unlock the door.

   The palm of his hand hit the window.

   I hit the unlock button twice, again, again.


He slid in, smiling at me awkwardly, put the two coffees in the holders.

   –I got us sandwiches. Here. And I got you a cookie.

   I stuffed the plastic wrapper in the glove compartment, a habit Tova hated.

   He chewed quietly.

   Chilled bread and meat, wilted lettuce, mayonnaise, salt.

   –Thanks.

–So there's just a couple more places on the list. You OK?

–Yeah.

–Is it still OK for you to drive me to get the rest of the stuff?

–Yeah. Sure. Yeah.

–It's just a place at UBC. Those condos at the other end of campus.

–More rich people.

–It's just about who can give stuff away, I guess.

–You have a bed? We're not picking up a bed.

–This is weird, but Quinn's mom called me and offered me an old futon she was going to throw away. She brought it over. She brought me two pans of lasagna. She made me promise I wasn't smoking pot and doing my meds at the same time.

I laughed.

–It was embarrassing. I didn't know she even knew.

–William. Everybody knew.

He nodded, chewed his sandwich. I took the lid off my coffee and drank.

After he got out of the hospital the first time, he told me not to tell anyone where he'd been. Paler and much thinner, his eyes ringed in black, he told me to tell anyone who asked that he'd been at a meditation retreat. Somewhere enviable. The second stay, the third. It became a habit to call his and Kyle's apartment and, if no one picked up, immediately call the ward. The woman at the desk knew my voice. The best friend. Of no relation.

It was impossible to sleep in the hospital, he told me. There was always light coming from somewhere. Never darkness. In darkness, a patient might escape. In darkness, he might try to kill himself again. In darkness, he might already be dead. A round light embedded in the ceiling; the flashlight of a night nurse; the glow of a nightlight with no switch. It was all half-light; a half-world, nowhere, noplace. He drifted.

We drove up the hill to campus.

–Where is this place.

He repeated the address. The south end of campus had been filled with townhouses: red brick, white doors. A child's model of Boston. We circled the developments then crossed Marine Drive and drove down into the new, large settlement where the university had allowed a section of the forest to be torn out. Now there was a Save On Foods; a Blenz; housing for faculty and their families.

–Here we go.

A woman opened the door, one hand on the doorknob, her other arm around a baby.

–Hi I'm William. We spoke on the phone yesterday about picking up some stuff you put on the Net?

–Oh right. That isn't me. That's our tenant. She has the basement suite. Door around the side, at the back.

–Thanks.

We walked along the sculpted gravel path. A woman around my age opened the door. Her face still red from the heat of the shower, hair wet and slung heavily back.

–You William?

–Yeah.

–Hey, I'm Jen. All the stuff's there on the couch.

As I stepped inside, the smell of pot overwhelmed me. I coughed and William inhaled.

The couch was covered in junk. I saw the Buddha lamp;

and a box of unused three-ring binders; a shopping bag full of stuffed animals; a fold-up picnic chair; a gas mask; a microwave tilted on a snowdrift of paperbacks.

–You said you had a space heater.

She shrugged.

–Sorry, I think I still need it.

–You put it on the list.

–Look. Leave the crap, okay? I don't care. I was just trying to do a good thing. I don't care. I'll just put it in the landfill if you don't want it.

She spoke with the stilted, leering rhythm of someone on a bad high. Had she been smoking up in the shower?

She caught me staring at the gas mask.

–Oh I got that off eBay. It's Israeli. Someone was selling it for ten bucks.

–Seriously?

–Yeah. I'm getting rid of all that stuff. Take whatever you want.

William was already at the couch, sorting through the paperbacks. *Oh my God porn* he mouthed to me across the room.

–God I can't wait to get out of this dump.

–You're moving?

–Yeah. Montreal.

–Oh, great.

–You from here?

–Yeah.

–Yeah me too. No one ever leaves Vancouver.

–Really? I know lots of people who've left.

–Yeah, but they come back, right?

–I don't know.

But it was true. I still saw my classmates from kindergarten at concerts. Several people I'd been to high school with had become managers of Starbucks in different neighbourhoods. Most of them had gone to UBC for their undergrad; some had moved away for grad school or to travel; and then they returned. Back in Van, they shrugged, as if it had happened by accident.

–Why Montreal?

–A friend lives there, I'm moving in with her. I want to learn French.

–Cool.

William held up a box of rusted metal objects.

–What're these?

–Railway spikes. Found them on a hike on the island. Thought it was cool at the time. That's where the old railway used to be. But I can't drag all this old crap around with me forever.

–They won't let you take railway spikes on the plane anyway.

Her laughter lasted for several minutes; too long. William stared at her. Jen put a hand on my shoulder.

–Railway spikes on an airplane. Railway spikes on an airplane.

William started putting things inside the microwave. A few of the books; a cheese grater; the railway spikes. He looped the gas mask around his neck.

–So you guys are moving in together?

William laughed.

–No. I'm just helping him move. He just got back to town.

–Where were you?

–Edmonton.

–School?

He shrugged.

–Just stuff. Working.

–What kind of work?

–I'm a doctor.

She raised her eyebrows and said nothing. She took a joint out of the pocket of her hoodie, lit it and took a long drag. She offered it to me.

–We have to get going. William.

I jammed the flat-screen TV in beside the desk and forced the microwave onto the back seat. We piled in the picnic chair and the rest of Jen's stuff.

–I wish you hadn't taken the gas mask.

–Why?

–Because it belonged to someone. It's a gas mask.

–But she got it off EBay.

–It's from Israel. Someone wore that.

It hung limply against his chest, an empty staring face.

–It's just a thing. Who cares?

–She shouldn't have had that.

The mask was made of thick black rubber, with five buckles stretching back around the skull — two around each side and one above the forehead — and a strap to loop around the wearer's neck. Large eye covers were inset, a pair of camera lenses, and the black rubber curved up around them, making the facial area of the mask a swollen space for the eyes, then a sharp curve to the beak or nose and the heavy filter the diameter of a soup can. The head behind the edge of the mask would be exposed. William took it off and threw it into the car on top of the Buddha lamp. Their sudden pairing; curves in common, thick surfaces. I slammed the door.

Light lurking in the trees, the moss and pathways darkening. Evening, already. UBC was on a peninsula, twin to Stanley

Park. Darkness always came here swift and complete, nothing but the ocean holding back the light.

His building in Yaletown was new but old; built in the 90s and rapidly graying, probably leaking. The elevator shaft groaned, a sick throat we drifted up.

One of his roommates was watching the Food Network. She looked me over and said hello with a strong Japanese accent.

–Hi.

–Hello William.

–How was your day.

–Good.

–We just have some stuff for my room so we'll be hauling things for half an hour. Sorry about the noise. I promise it won't take long. I just needed stuff for my room. We spent the day driving around all over the place getting it.

She nodded; I could tell she hadn't understood what he'd said.

–I'm Laura.

–Sister?

–Friend.

–Oh. Friend.

From the way she looked at me, skeptically, I knew that I was the first person William had brought over since becoming her roommate. I smiled. I wondered what she had seen of him over the past few weeks. Was William able to sleep now? Did he push the days without pills?

William opened a door at the other end of the living room and stared at me expectantly.

–Good-bye.

–Good-bye. Nice meet you.

His room was small. A large window in one wall. The room was empty except for the futon from Quinn's mother, a small stack of books, an open suitcase and backpack full of clothes. His laptop nested in the quilt on the futon.

We took turns holding doors and carrying the day's objects.

He tilted the flat screen against a wall and put the bean-bag chair in front of it. The VCR, the box of cassettes. The desk against the opposite wall and the fold-out chair in front of it. The Buddha lamp on the floor beside the paperbacks and the futon. The microwave in the corner under the window. I watched him arrange the railway spikes in a row on the windowsill, small sculptures of rust and shadow. Dust gradually orbited.

He dug through his backpack and took out four bottles of pills and, crouching, tipped one pill from each bottle into his pocketed hand and swallowed them dry.

I fell onto the futon. Exhaustion stretched my legs out.

Lying down, I watched him hurry around the room, straightening and adjusting things. His white-winged hands moving the way they always did, precise and nervous, nothing ever quite right, in need of adjustment invisible to everyone else. When I'd first met him he'd taken me on daylong expeditions through vintage clothing shops in downtown Vancouver; always in basements, always smelling of leather and mothballs. Look, he'd gush, and hold a hat or a scarf. This is perfect. A day not long before the first hospital stay we were sitting in the cement stairwell leading down to the food court under the student union building and he doubled over, held his hands over his elbows. I'm fooling everyone, he said. I've been fooling everyone. You're the only one who knows me, he said. Sometimes it scares me, you know, that there's another me walking around. A me? Another me, you. I'm not you, William. No. He was wearing a blue-and-green plaid cotton jacket, a black polo shirt for contrast, jeans rippled in a dark wash, polished boots, a scarf wide and soft as a pashmina shawl. He scratched at the sleeves, as if trying to tear through the fabric. What is this. What is this.

– Can I make you some tea?

– No, I'm good.

– Okay. I'm just going to make some for myself.

The door opened and shut.

Water gushing into the kettle. The Food Network blaring the play-by-play of a kitchen battle. Footsteps overhead. Distantly, the elevator. The thin-walled building talking to itself.

A weak scream.

I ran into the living room.

The roommate was sitting on the couch, her hands over her face. William stood in the doorway to the kitchen, holding the kettle up, wearing the gas mask.

The heavy eyes stared at me. The straps dividing the skull into neat sections; the nose of a soldier or insect. I heard a sound like choking, a rhythmic sucking. I stepped forward. But it was only his laughter.

The other two roommates came home and I stood aside as William showed them his room. They nodded; one of them touched the railway spikes. I loathed their bemusement. They did not know how much this was, for him, to make one room.

I tell you this: watching him lose his mind was watching him burn alive.

Across the Burrard bridge to Kits, the inside of Pacific's dark arm.

Let the car drift into the silent grid of streets, even calm turns.

Into the parking lot above the sand. At eye level, the water moved outward.

Something moved gently against my foot. A stray paperback Harlequin from that troll, Jen. I opened the window and hurled it out onto pavement.

Was this beach where he did it? I never knew which beach it was. When Kyle had called, he'd repeated, he was on the beach, he was on the beach. The hospital had called. A taxi driver doing a sweep for drunken teenagers needing rides had seen him on the sand. Unconscious, but thank God he was so skinny and the taxi driver was a strong guy in his forties, a Russian accent, Kyle told me when he took him out for lunch months afterward to say thank you. It was the bright jacket that saved him, the taxi driver told Kyle. The yellow jacket William liked to wear over everything, anything. Sometimes people fell asleep on the beach but the taxi driver knew something was wrong when he touched William's back and he was soaking wet.

–Why did you come back out of the water, I'd asked him in the hospital.

The water was colder than he'd expected. The liquor he'd drunk after taking all his pills wasn't enough to generate warmth. Windy. He couldn't swim. Terror of sinking. Wasn't that why he went out there in the first place, to sink? Once he was there it was too cold. He'd turned around.

Was it this beach? Spanish Banks, Jericho, English Bay, Kits beach. Those are the beaches in Vancouver where a driver can see a body from the road.

A week later I hadn't heard from him. He answered the phone, voice thick, too early to call he said, didn't I know he was jobless and single. How was the stuff working out? Did the microwave work? Yes, and the Buddha lamp, he paused, has a second light bulb in its stomach. He was keeping a list of free things I would like. Boxes of disposable razor blades and a quaint wooden bassinette. Vintage library cards from someone's grandmother's library catalogue. A glass punch bowl with eight cups. There was no end to what people were willing to give away if someone else would do all the work for them. Someone had posted thirty pounds of frozen dog food; pick it up before it starts to thaw. A woman wanted to get rid of her ex's stamp collection. It was worth thousands but she would burn it rather than sell it, so would someone please just come and take it away from her.

Quinn's mother found him a job shelving books at the library; her friend was the head librarian. He didn't have to talk to anybody.

He paused.

–I watched the tapes.

–Tapes?

–That we got with the VCR.

–All of them?

–Yeah. I wasn't feeling like going out for a few days. I watched all of them.

–How many were there.

–I don't know. Years. It was like watching a whole series on DVD all at once. Two sets of kids. Remember there were kids' toys in the house? There're older kids on the tapes too. I guess he was married before.

–Well no one uses tapes anymore.

–Yeah. This was his old family I think.

–So what kind of stuff was there?

–You know, like, family stuff. Picnics and soccer games. Christmas.

–You watched their Christmases?

–Yeah. I wasn't feeling well. I don't know, it kept me company.

Would I drive him around again sometime? There was some more stuff he needed. He needed a pillow and a bedside table for his books and his mother had sent him some money to buy new clothes for work. This time, he promised, it wouldn't be like last time. He wouldn't do what he'd done last time. He had a list. He was organized. This time we would go to stores and buy things; this time there would be no strangers.

I pictured him in his room, surrounded by the collection of haphazard treasures. Watching each video, following it with another. That huge flat screen TV in that small room. The enactment of family rituals. Children he had never met unwrapping presents ten years ago. A couple waving from a picnic table. Kyle, he said, wasn't answering his calls. Stop calling, I said, he's never going to answer, he's gone now. Quinn was going to take him out to a bar, maybe he would meet someone new, he said. But eventually they'll find out who I am, he said. Yes they will, I said. Yes they will.

# PEOPLE WHO ARE MICHAEL

**THIS IS THE FIRST VIDEO** Michael uploads to his channel.

Michael stands in front of the Bart Simpson poster in his bedroom. You can see that the room is small. Flood of white-washed palm as he reaches out to adjust the webcam. He steps back. His confidence balanced on one foot. He gives you one smile. *Hey YouTube this is Michael's channel you probably know this song already.* High soft-toned voice. Not yet broken. Small-boned for his age.

The bass begins. Woolly beats embedded in the computer. Behind the webcam's eye, drifting from your speakers. Michael nods seriously, agreeing to the rhythm. His first sung broadcast words: *I need you.*

Michael angles his face downward, hair sliding to shield his erratic eyelids that flicker, like snare rimshots, like REM sleep cycles. He fiddles with his thin gold necklace. His fingers rest on the neckline of his grey T-shirt, then his palm floats over his chest, taps at his stomach.

When he gets to the chorus Michael looks into the camera for the first time.

Into your eye and something in his throat has opened. The notes slip an octave, effortless, in time, a glide that stuns.

*Oh I gotta have you.* Voice tripping high, startled by the key change.

Michael's head slides to the side, his eyes switch from the lens to someone else behind the camera, his mother or an audience in the music video he imagines. Shades of grey and gold in his dark eyes, he is eyeing the ceiling, lungs swelled, a fist throwing false punches midair where he imagines drums. When he hunches his shoulders are unbelievably narrow. A swimmer's pounce to the last verse.

You look closely at the beige wall behind him, the brown couch the size and height of a bench, the anonymous carpet.

The oversized softness of his ears under scattered hair inked with sweat. *I need you I need you I need you-you-you. Ooooooh.*

Winner's slouch off-screen, a close-up of his smile. Satisfaction. He presses the necessary button to vanish.

• • •

White-and-red palm over an iPhone's spider eye. The fan holding the iPhone breathing. *It's him it's him oh my God.*

Michael in dark glinting jeans and a turquoise hoodie. Walking swiftly, head down, a security guard for each part of his stride. Then he's pulled through the rear door of a black van. The blur of him. You see how he holds his hand over the side of his face and the way his back curves as he slides into the seat. The screams that chase him into the van.

Fluorescent sky, freewheeling. Somewhere in summer, a bleached screen's false heatwave, in the middle of his second European tour, you squint to make out flesh and metal as the iPhone is dropped.

Clattering at the hard edges of the picture. *Michael I love you.*

The security guard's face, relaxed smile-lines. *He's gone girls.* Then the smash against pavement. The security guard's boot. The percussive hysteria of the girls. *Fuck you man.* The van speeding away. An engine is buried in the screaming of the girls. Screen in motion, the antlered light.

The last frame of the video is a close-up of the security guard's cheek. The screen moves like one muscle.

*Michael will you marry me* shouted to an electric field of cascading static, to the overexposed sky.

. . .

The video is shot from a distance. The image foggy, possibly filmed through a window. Michael sits in an airport lounge. He's in normal clothes, not the kind he wears in photos. Flip-flops show his pale feet; grey sweatpants; a black T-shirt; a jean jacket. Michael at thirteen or fourteen. A plainclothes security guard sits beside him. You can tell he's a guard from the neutral fixedness of his stare, his mirrored sunglasses, the set of his shoulders. Michael crosses his ankles, chews slowly, eyes blank. He yawns, cups a hand over his mouth, continues chewing. No luggage sits around them and no other travellers are visible. FLY HORIZON is printed in red letters across the wall behind Michael. The image zooms in closer to Michael, drifts over his shoulder. Two more security guards stand against the wall, to the right of HORIZON. Michael takes his phone out of his pocket and begins to finger the keypad. The image holds steady. An inspection, a cold recording, not a fan video — those always jerk and sway with excitement. Michael sits still, focused on his phone. Playing a game? Texting a friend? His face blank. Then, slowly, his eyes move from the phone's screen. He is looking directly at the camera, directly at you. He's found you. No, you realize, he's known the whole time. You expect the autopilot bright-light smile but there is none. His stare is level and static. You want to stop watching but you can't. Looking at you, Michael stops chewing. He takes his gum from his mouth and says a word. The security guard sitting beside him puts out his hand. Michael puts the gum in the guard's hand who then walks off the screen, returns. Michael continues to look at you. *Stop it,* Michael mouths. The video continues for thirteen minutes. *Stop it,* he mouths again. Michael does not look away from you.

· · ·

A morning show interview someone has uploaded: a video of the TV screen. The hazy darkness of someone's living room around the image. Kitchen sounds from off-screen. First a cartoon of a sunny-side egg and the host's face floating in the yolk. *Hi Philadelphia.* The jingle.

Then Michael in white jeans, a heavy silver belt buckle pushed to the right of centre, a form-fitting sweater unzipped over a v-neck shirt, his hair molded to his narrow head. The interviewer in a pencil skirt, sitting at thirty-degree angles to Michael and the camera. Michael in a fashionable classroom slouch. He straightens up.

*So you were discovered on your YouTube channel. Did you expect this kind of success?*

*Uh yeah, no, on Youtube, no, this has been really crazy, you know, coming from a small town in Canada, I'm just really glad, just really honoured by all the fans and the attention, you know.*

*It's an amazing story.*

*Yeah the producer found my videos cuz I sang a cover of one of his singer's songs and flew us down to* LA.

Michael smiles through the questions. Teeth bared, eyes ready. Doe-eyed, the columnists call him; deer in the headlights, sometimes. Michael blinks. His blink is his trademark now, has been the subject of editorials in national newspapers and fold-out posters in all the teen heartthrob glossies. From his first YouTube videos, that shimmer, part hesitation, part flash, they write.

The host is a woman a decade younger than his mother and Michael fits his smiles to her questions until she is motherly, encouraging, suggests words to fill out his choppy answers. *So it's been a year since you posted those first videos, how does it feel to not be able to walk down the street without being recognized?*

Michael looks at you, holds up a hand, flips a peace sign,

lets his hand crumple like a leaf in a small sudden fire. *I owe it all to my fans.*

*How have you dealt with all the attention?* Michael talks about his crew that is his new family, his mother who always travels with him, the R&B artist who signed him and is like a *father, I mean like a mentor to me, he's just always reminding me to stay humble. And my swagger coach, that helps too.*

The host laughs. *Swagger coach?*

Michael laughs. You look closer, see his embarrassment start.

*Yeah, you know, he, you know, shows me how to be smooth and stuff.*

*You mean a stylist.*

*Yeah yeah, a stylist.*

Michael slides down the leather studio couch, crosses his high-tops — silver and plum to match his sweater. He observes the camera angle travelling, twists his legs to reciprocate and to show you his new shoes, the patterns on their sides like lacquered feathers. *It's cool, it's all good, just appreciating, just appreciating.*

The interviewer smiles and Michael smiles. He is perfect in that picturelock moment, and she is another adult in front of whom he has melted and slipped by.

*So tell me about starting your YouTube channel.*

A shot of a girl in the audience, wearing sunglasses. The left lens reads MICH in white-out. The right lens reads AEL.

*Well singing was just something I always did, brushing my teeth, in church, at family picnics and stuff you know and in my bedroom and I started a YouTube channel just for fun, you know, just something to do, most of my friends did like online diary stuff like talking about movies and their classes so I thought I'd just sing.*

Teeth. Timing.

He blinks. Not a blink to mask the water surface of eyes, you notice, but a long blink. Staged short-circuiting of his famous eyes. Michael believes that he is sending messages with his eyes. You are watching Michael's eyes, all of these videos, for messages.

*Please come by again Michael good luck with the tour. Thank you. No thank you, thank you.*

Michael's new single fades in. Heavy bass and his autotuned voice singing an arpeggio over the liquid guitars.

As the music cranks up, the camera pans the studio audience, rows of silent watching girls who now, released, finally, can begin to scream.

.   .   .

The choppy thrash of a minicam's mic battling wind. You squint at the bleached picture until the light separates into forms and Michael becomes clear. A cricket Michael, legs reaching bent from a tall stool, the guitar gigantic in his arms, the outdoor stage showing its metal braces. *Um, this is a song by Sarah McLachlan, yeah, um, here it is.* Aluminum sky. Bleachers scattered with people picnicking.

The comment below the video: *Michael before he was famous . . . sorry about the video quality . . . you can hear his voice pretty great though . . . ignore my kids screaming in the background they wanted hot dogs as you can probably tell* LOL.

The wind raises and drops sheets of static.

Michael's arms cradle and struggle against the guitar. His head bent. He studies his fingers on the strings, preparing for the combination of sounds he will make. His huge white sneakers dangle like sunspots on the fuzzy image.

A backwards baseball cap too big for his head — blown off by the wind, sent tumbling across the stage. Michael watches its panicked dance.

The minicam's long shaky zoom, the squarish pixels of Michael's pink cheeks, an abstract mosaic. The audio persists purely. White-blond hair. Michael at ten, eleven? His voice slices the distortion of the picture. The guitar dwarfs him, a hollow bright pine buoy he is grasping.

He repeats the intro, begins the song on an off-beat, recovers. His voice staggers through the first verse.

He starts the chorus, then startles at the cry that splits the soft grey air an inch from the minicam's mic: *Moooooooom hot dooog hot dog hot dog.*

The image zooms out.

You catch a glimpse of the heavy plastic watch on his wrist, the kind a kid could win from an arcade machine at a movie theatre. You are looking at the watch because Michael is watching it carefully. He is using the watch to keep time. *Mom mom mom hot dog.*

The picture plunges. A child's eye. Accusing you. Four black finger-stripes across the screen. You are pulled downward, against the words blasted by her huge lips. Michael's voice now just an electric background whisper. *Mom. Hot dog. Now.*

· · ·

A slide show of photos of Michael compiled by his mother after his disappearance. Uploaded to his music label's YouTube channel — then it goes viral across all the fan channels.

The line of text running along the bottom of the photos: *Michael if you are watching this I love you.* REWARD REWARD REWARD. Each photo stays on the screen for ten seconds. Things that could be used to identify Michael. Things to identify the most YouTubed person in the world, you think.

The birthmark on the right side of his neck.

The joint of his right pinky, which is crooked.

The small-print tattoo he got on his sixteenth birthday, just over a year ago, on the inside of his right arm, his microphone arm: Perfect Pitch Is A Curse.

Three conjoined photos of him in each of his three favourite hoodies.

A close-up of the silver bracelet he always wears on his left wrist.

·  ·  ·

Michael wet, slipping out of the Australian ocean, the flash of cameras from the beach, the hot flash of the sand, the studio beauty of his after-swim smile, a girl shouting *Oh my God he isn't wearing a shirt!* He steps forward, leg bent flexibly out, so they can catch him in mid-stride. The camera light shines off the salt on his skin. The light is a shining hood he sheds. This video is thirteen seconds long.

·  ·  ·

The radiant screens of phones held up, recording, a frantic star chart. A stadium venue. This phone recording the shaky, blaring video is one of hundreds. The noise billowing off the crowd. The phone cracked open by the speaker system and thousands of screamers. Struggling to stay on that one moving spot on the stage — Michael in white.

Michael's shape burned white in the darkness, streaming rays of motion, Michael leaping onto an amp, leaping off and landing mid-run, the chorus chasing him up the runway built over the audience. Footwork, weavebacks on downbeats. *Oooh you are all I want and want and want.* Darkness.

The camera pans the stadium for a moment. A rippling silvery valley lined with bodies. A roar pierced by *I love you Michael* and the siren cry *Marry me.* How can he sing to each of them.

Small lights.

Each person holds their phone up like a candle.

The picture skims shoulders and heads back to the stage.

She. Michael's arm reaching down from the stage. One fan, chosen, pulled out of the sea.

You turn the volume down on your computer, the scream is so sheer, so total. One scream.

She — barely standing, holding her head. Michael cradles her elbow in overstated public tenderness, circles her, half a moonwalk and back around her, popping up behind one shoulder, a cute trick from a home video, the microphone held in front of her mouth and she brays the lyrics she has known for months. *You and me for-evah and evah girl.* Her hands up over her mouth and eyes. Michael leads her across the stage and she vanishes — a larger shape, a security guard, is waiting to escort her to an exit.

Michael sprints back to the centre of the stage, arms spread-eagled, head down, and everyone has forgotten the girl by the time he reaches the centre. They want to forget her so he will sing to them, to you, again.

The song ends. The silence is loudest. The thumping space hollowed out by the speakers. Michael raises his arms, gives you two peace signs. The one scream again.

The screen above the stage that shows the close-up of Michael shows his blink, his smile. He crosses his arms and poses at an angle, a child's *Come on impress me* pose. His sixteen-year-old face dominates the arena. The one scream — the roof is made of sound and it is breaking.

Michael kneels and unlaces his left shoe. He balls the lace up in his hand and throws it. Radiant string.

The first of the crowd speeds through the loose line of security. Then ten girls, then thirty. Over the lip of the stage. The screen shows Michael's arms fall, then his hands go up flat, No Stop. His speaking voice, once in the mic: *No don't please.* The hard sound of the live mic hitting the stage when he drops it. Turns to run. As security emerges from the wings, Michael is tackled at the knees by a girl.

He folds.

The guards come up against the girls, pull them off Michael, toss them easily forward. The crowd roars, as if this is wrestling, a part of the show. The guards move forward, eight of them, in formation. Where is Michael? You look. A bright smudge on the stage, pressed to it. A spotlight, a bright hole.

The bass intro for the next song starts. Michael is a white ball of light carried offstage between three guards.

When the phone's eye sweeps back again, the crowd is silenced.

The phone is turned around and you see the person who

has recorded this video for you: a boy, twelve or thirteen, wearing a white V-neck T-shirt and two silver wings on a chain. His short bleached hair. *If one of you assholes who rushed the stage watch this I want you know you ruined it for everybody.* The image wavers, his hand trembling. *We all love Michael and you ruined it for everybody.* His smooth lips pinch. His eyes contemptuous. *I love him and you ruined it.* Around him the stadium lights come up. A thunder of disappointment rises. *I love him.*

    *Michael Michael Michael Michael.* The chanting shakes the air. The video ends.

· · ·

Is that neck or light curve. Slide of stomach or a blanket around a limb, a curtain pulling the lens past the shadow's shoulder line.

    Breath.

    Beginning of arm.

    Your low-resolution eye. The points of three white knuckles, or toes floating upward, two bodies going under like a burial at sea, slipping under a sheer surface. Polished surface or lightless surface, pressed together. Breath, hard. A microphone cries. Michael chuckles. And under.

    The back of his head, hair sways forward.

    *Where are you. No there.* You can tell from the note in his voice that he does not know that this is being recorded. Strained, weakening. *Oh God.*

    A female voice sings a line from Michael's first single, the one he recorded when he was thirteen, the first to hit No.1. *No,* he moans. *I hate that fucking song.*

    The lens molts shadow, gains ground on skin.

Background grid, high-up window, the faint silver of overcast sky, the roof of a metal world.

You glance at the number: 7,523,418 views since the video was uploaded a week ago.

The rim of the picture drifts. Eyeswitch of angle. *Oh. There.*

The camera drags, a finger at Michael's waist.

Retaliation, quiet plunge of laughter, this is Michael's neck, white open shoulders. This is before the placement of cold glass over his white specimen chest. Because it is skin that lets.

Part of a forehead, a wide eye. The back of Michael's head bright, blocking the light from her chest. Her eye on yours.

. . .

The first video Michael uploads after his disappearance.

*This video isn't for you,* he says.

A plain room around him, in a hotel or not, a room that could be anywhere.

*I just want my mom to know I'm* OK.

He should look emaciated, starved. Kidnapped, as the headlines have said. A millionaire many times over, a few months older than seventeen. He blinks. Calm forehead, white shirt. He leans forward. The video ends.

. . .

In this video Michael speaks to you directly. Today is the release date for his second album.

Michael's face fills most of the screen. Behind his shoulders, a white-and-contrast-cream hotel room, a stripe of industrial sky. Michael speaks quickly, his eyes on yours. *I just want to uh thank you guys for everything, this all happened because of you guys, I owe it all to my fans.*

You notice the bluish semi-circle below each of Michael's eyes. The fine net of light tethered to his skin. The near translucence of his eyelids and core white of his teeth. The ticking silence of the hotel room.

*Wow the millions of uh hits I just couldn't have imagined this could have ever, like, happened to me, just a regular guy you know. When I started this channel like just over two years ago.* His voice has broken. His voice is deeper. Since recording the songs on this album, most of which has been leaked to YouTube, his voice has changed into another version of itself. He got two albums in before his voice broke.

Michael leans back for a moment. Nostrils and eyelids so smooth, android from this angle.

The click-hush of a door opening and closing. A link appears across Michael's chest: BUY MY ALBUM ON ITUNES NOW!!!!!! A shadow moves behind Michael. The door opens and closes again. You wonder: his mother? routine security sweep? Silence again.

Michael blinks. *Anyway I just wanted to say thankyou thankyou thankyou guys you're all amazing.* He reaches forward. The screen goes black and fades to an ad for the album. You click on the iTunes link.

• • •

Michael standing in the glow of a large hotel bathroom. He looks into the mirror. *Hey Much Music this is my tour diary thanks for watching! This going to be so much fun!* He brushes his teeth and spits into the marble sink.

. . .

Wide cement steps leading to a theatre. Michael sits on the top step. The video is clear and steady. A day without wind. Blue light, evening. His guitar case is open on the sidewalk. He is singing. Snaps his shoulders side-to-side. His sneakers add dull-edged syncopation. A Coke can on the step below him. A gospel song.

He plays to the camera, without looking at it. The obliviousness and bravado of an experienced busker. The person holding the camera speaks to someone near by, her voice rasping on the mic: *This child is my hero he's here like every day. You're my hero little genius child!*

Michael switches tempo into an R&B song. He sings: *Oh I gotta stop thinking about having my first chile.* Laughter. *Chile you planning on having a chile?* Michael tilts his face, mouth and eyes clenched with emotion: *ooooooh girl can't stop thinking of you.* He bears down on the downbeat.

A small audience gathers on the steps around Michael. A woman in her thirties sits next to him, arms looped around her knees. Her face blank as she watches him. She takes large bites from her hot dog. She chews slowly.

A shout from off-screen: *Kid hey how about some Joni Mitchell. No Jay-Z. Jay-Z kid.*

*Isn't it past your bedtime kid.*

Michael sings a verse of Joni. He yells *Switch.* Then screams out Jay-Z.

*Oh kid's got game.*

Laughter. Taunting, admiring.

Coins and bills fill his guitar case.

In profile, Michael's jaw works and flexes. Chewing the words.

The song-pulse prodding his neck from the inside.

He presses one finger into the centre of his audience. Belts a slowjam chorus over their heads. Coins thrown.

Light wind tosses Michael's hair across his eyes.

*Switch,* a man yells, *Hallelujah.*

*The Rufus Wainwright version or the Leonard Cohen one,* Michael says.

Throttle-sound of laughter flooding the mic.

*You choose kid.*

He sings Leonard Cohen's version. A hoot from the crowd. The crying of wheels. *Hallelujah*

*Halle*

*lujaaaaaah.*

It begins to rain softly and the crowd moves onto the steps, which are protected by an overhang off-screen. The camera now films Michael from the side. A man crosses his legs, lights a cigarette, sits with his head dangling. His head moves back and forth, a long shadow moving like a minute hand over Michael's sneakers. *How'd you get to be so old kid.* A seagull lands on the top step. Michael must be from a town near the ocean. You've never thought before about where Michael might be from. Dark now, Michael and his audience ghosts sketched in the night, touches of street light from beyond the edges of the steps. *Shit my battery's dying shit shit shit.* The image streaked with white regions that flow, the audio fluxing, Michael's final *hallelujah* an interrupted moan. The sound of a can opener turning, working. Chords turn their soft-sided wheels. The video cuts out as Michael begins the Rufus Wainwright cover.

. . .

Michael stepping through the open sliding glass door of a hotel room onto a balcony. A blast of screams that the camera moves toward. A city square below, crowded with women, a black perimeter of cops, visors pulled up and glinting, riot gear, a reflective sunset of plastic shields. Someone speaks rapid German in the background — a reporter, you assume. Two security guards, one for each of Michael's eyes, feet, arms, knees, as he moves toward the edge of the balcony. His red-and-yellow checkered boots tie into the amber and cherry tones of his smoker's jacket, ironic and loose-fitting over a black v-neck shirt. Another guard is already standing at the balcony railing. Michael reaches out and takes the megaphone out of his hand. The guard looks surprised, then nods, moves quickly around Michael and into position with the two other guards and the small crowd that has emerged from the hotel room: Michael's mother, his manager, a few others you imagine are producers or assistants. They hang back as Michael paces the balcony railing, holding the megaphone. He puts a finger to his lips, looking down at the crowd, its shrieking. *Shhhhhhhhhhh*. He moves the finger out and then softly replaces it to his lips.

The crowd stills.

*Oh I need you*, Michael sings. Acapella for the first time in years. The first time you've seen since those first videos.

His voice blurts harshly through the megaphone. *Oh yeah.
I need you girl.*

The crowd screams. Stills. The boundary of police take
one step in as the crowd moves closer to the balcony. Michael
doesn't move.

*Marry me Michael.*

He's fourteen or fifteen in this video. His shoulders have
filled out a bit.

*Come and get me,* he speaks back — the megaphone thundering his voice.

One scream.

A security guard moves forward and stands at the railing,
scans the crowd for snipers. He taps Michael's shoulder and
Michael grins at him, shouts lyrics into the megaphone again.
The security guard extends one hand and wraps his fingers
around Michael's wrist. Michael begins to struggle — sudden,
fish-like movements, a full-body snap from his stomach to his
knees. His mother rushes forward and leads him back into the
hotel. He goes. The guard who held him follows. Michael turns
suddenly and blasts painfully into the guard's face: *Baby.*

The guard staggers back, steps forward. Michael runs into
the hotel, waving the megaphone like a small flag, laughing.
Sprints into the building. Retaliation saved until he reaches
open space.

The guard follows.

Then turns, holds a hand over the camera. The broad palm
cancels all light as it draws closer, before covering everything.

. . .

Dim gold light of a recording booth. Michael in a white T-shirt and the thin gold necklace from his first uploads. Beyond the booth's window, the figures of men. Michael's head clenched between the oversized ears of his headphones. The bass line leaking out, his voice naked as he sings his lines over the playback into the mic. One of the men raises his hand. Michael nods. Brief silence and he begins nodding to the beat. *You and me*, he sings. The man raises his hand again and Michael stops. Silence, again, then the music starts and Michael starts. This is repeated twelve times. Michael continues the thirteenth time, his body inside the song's lockstep harmonies. *One more time,* a piped voice states. *A third higher. Yeah sure,* Michael says. This is recorded once, approved with a wave from beyond the glass. Syncopation in Michael's finger joints, played against his waist. *No I didn't get that at the end,* Michael says. *What Mike?* Michael shakes his head: *It wasn't right.* OK *one more time then.* After this repetition Michael slides his headphones off, drops them, lets them dangle. *Perfect*, Michael says. His voice cracks. A jump in the middle of perfect. A break. Michael shakes his head violently. The men behind the glass laugh. *Per-fect,* they mimic. *Per-yeee-fect.* Michael turns and you see his face for the first time. Eyes nakedly red from the session's focus. He blinks, stunned, at you, surprised to find you here, too.

. . .

The last video Michael uploads after his disappearance. He has been gone for nine months.

His hands. The police confirm that those are in fact his

hands. His hands opening and closing. Occasionally, breathing can be heard in the background.

You watch his hands. Where they would grasp the microphone.

His hands opening, closing. Because it is the last video, it is watched by everyone. Twenty-two million views, then more, more, the most viewed video.

His hands open and close. You watch this video again, again. For the same reason that you watched every other video of Michael: because you love him.

The opening and closing of his hands, a steady rhythm, cupping and revealing something you cannot quite see, you think, looking closer.

Shadows in the creases at his knuckles, but that is all.

This video is eighteen minutes long.

# TWO-HANDED THINGS

**LEARNING TO TIE A SLING**

The scream from the black ice below the bedroom window. Then silence and Kim, deep in her duvet cocoon, thinks, was it a jagged piece of wind slicing into the December sky, or a frozen tree snapping, dark needled head ploughing into white? — it's Amanda oh my God it's Amanda — and the duvet follows Kim as she struggles down the stairs, moves toward the screams.

That frail line on the backlit x-ray. Kim looks at the inside of Amanda's wrist. Bone glows moon-pure against the black hollowness of blood. The tiny fissure. A faint road on a bleached-out map.

The doctor explains that bones knit to heal. Lunate fracture. Her trained hands prod the swollen area. Eyes closed, she is silent. Kim realizes that she is picturing the bones.

– Can I drive? Amanda asks.

– Bend your fingers for me. Again?

The doctor shows Amanda how to tie her sling.

– People who might have to help with this might want to be watching how to do this, the doctor says, and Kim rushes over like a kid. The doctor ties and unties the sling three times. Kim memorizes how the fabric slides and wraps at the elbow.

– You'll be my right hand, Amanda says in the taxi back to their house.

Oh God, Kim thinks. The overwhelming number of necessary things.

– Whatever you need, she says.

Amanda starts her list. Her brain is a capable muscle, a planner for the world. Typing. What about showering? Putting on pants. Belts. Jewellery. Shoelaces . . . she has slip-ons. Opening envelopes. Kim does not make the joke about one hand clapping.

– It'll be like living in kindergarten, Amanda says. Practising finger snaps.

– We have three hands between us now. More than before, kind of.

Kim knows that this is something to say in an emergency, a warm half-truth. She knows this as she says it.

It would be better and easier if Kim had been the one to fall, but neither says this.

Half of Amanda's face goes crooked, her lips pressed and rippled as if her mouth is wired shut.

–I'm fine, it's fine. No, I'm fine.

At home, Amanda holds an ice pack to the plaster. Kim takes the ice pack in her good right hand and they stand near each other until Amanda believes that she feels the cold through the cast, a soothing whiteness against the bone.

**BUTTONING A SHIRT**

–Having trouble with that?

–I only ever do up buttons for myself, Kim says.

Kim's fingertips struggle with the buttons on Amanda's work blazer. Good buttons, flat and sleek.

–Like trying to fit something round through a round hole, Amanda says.

–Your buttons are different from mine. These are suit buttons.

–I have two shirts with snaps, Amanda says. Slip-on shoes, velcro on my gortex jacket, oh shit what about can openers?

–Stay still.

Every day, they have to wake up an hour earlier than usual to have time for all the two-handed things. It's only a few days since the fall, but it feels like weeks. When Kim brushes the cast, Amanda shrinks as if the white plaster is burned skin.

–Done.

–Can you do up my belt? I got it through the loops on my own.

Kim slides the belt's end through the buckle, cinches it in.

– Too tight, Amanda says.

– Sorry.

Kim shifts it a notch looser.

– Good.

Kim hears the opening in Amanda's voice. Last night she found her trying to open a jam jar in the kitchen, scraping at the hardened fruit glue that had sealed the lid. Kim took the jar, popped the lid. Amanda took it and threw it into the sink. Kim rinsed the spilled berries down the drain, went to bed to find Amanda shored up with pillows in bed. The outline of the cast under the quilt, an enlarged stronger bone. Moonlight thickening the white.

Kim has told her co-workers at Starbucks and the bookstore about the wrist and the cast and her friends have said, That doesn't sound so bad, She has you to help, That sounds like a pretty minor injury. Kim answered Yes, Yes, and Yes, but you don't know Amanda. Only Kim knows Amanda, she believes.

Amanda organized the kitchen, but Kim does all the cooking. Most of what they do is Amanda's plan, but Kim does all the talking.

– Do my collar, Amanda says. Please.

– Sure.

– No put it over the jacket collar.

– Like that?

– This is so humiliating.

– But I don't mind.

Kim wonders if this is how a parent feels. Coordination, precision, approbation. Performing endless hidden tasks.

Soon after they met, Amanda said, I became a teacher

because I hated being a kid, I hated not being able to do anything for myself. That was before they became lovers. That was
a little over five years ago.

They met at a friend's party. The friend said to Kim, Oh that's
Amanda, please just avoid her tonight, I want this party to be
fun, you'll hate each other, she's too intense for you. Sometimes
Kim remembers that and thinks, What if the friend was right?

Sometimes she wishes she'd been spared Amanda. Impecca-
ble taste — Kim had thought that was a cliché, before Amanda.
Since Amanda, Kim has avoided perfectly happy couples. Com-
patible hard drives napping against each other's warm bellies.
Love is easy for other people. Amanda is her flint, her net.

### PEELING A GRAPEFRUIT

Anything round is a problem. Without a flat surface, the thing
won't accept the knife's edge and path.

– It's about torque, Amanda says. With one hand, I have no
torque.

Amanda presses the knife. The fruit thumps onto the floor.

She laughs. Kim is relieved that Amanda can still laugh.
Amanda's jokes make Kim see the world dissected, backlit,
makes her hear the canned laughter of other people. Sometimes
Kim thinks: Amanda is bitter. Sometimes Kim thinks: No one
should have to see things that clearly.

– Just six weeks till the cast comes off, Kim says.

Amanda hunts the grapefruit across the floor, her knife
raised.

– Edward Scissorhands. Would you like me to peel your
grapefruit?

–Want to do it myself.

Amanda teaches elementary school. Yesterday she spent an hour telling Kim that the kids see the cast as a sign of weakness. Permission to treat her as prey. The girls offer to carry her books. The boys vanish like bugs between floorboards. Then the books are gone. Where are the books? The girls raise hands, offering names of suspects. Mozart. Dr. Phil. Alice Moonrow. The boys become twisting trails of laughter and shoe rubber. If Amanda moves quickly, a hot charge of pain surges. As if her arm is punishing her, Amanda says.

Amanda drives home from work every evening, exhausted, all of her energy drained out of the small space that has been opened in her.

Effort. Everything is now an effort.

Her colleagues do not help, she tells Kim. The men are not chivalrous. The women pretend not to see, the women joke that her cast does not match her scarf, the women are not nice at all but sideways and coded and more subtle than the men and the women and the women and the women.

Amanda is the only person Kim knows who has told her: I am self-made.

Kim grew up in a neighbourhood where people paid the neighbour's gardeners a little extra to prune the tubs of marigolds.

Amanda's family disowned her after she moved to this city. There were letters. The letters stopped. Kim knows that Amanda has never told her the whole story.

Kim says, Please, sweetie, I'll peel the grapefruit.

Amanda waves her hand No.

–I don't want it I'll have grapes forget it.

When Amanda said she was self-made, Kim thought, Doesn't everyone make their own self? Amanda told her that only rich people think that. She corrected herself: only people *born* rich think that. The world is against you if you can't do things for yourself.

The grapefruit lies on the floor. Amanda stands and splits red grapes with a paring knife, exposing the brilliant jewelled guts. This is enough for now.


**WRITING YOUR SIGNATURE**

–If it hadn't been my right wrist, Amanda says.

–If I hadn't gone out on deck, of course there was black ice, Amanda says.

–If black ice weren't invisible, Amanda says.

Amanda pushes away the paper covered in spikes and lines drifting into an exhausted alphabet. Crowds of crouched, pained words.

The pen slides from her swollen fingers.

–I can't do any of my normal things.

–Sorry.

–I need you to learn how to do my signature. I need it for work.

After Kim's first pages of attempts, Amanda says, You would make a horrible forger. You have honest hands. She reaches out and takes Kim's left hand.

Amanda's injured wrist is getting stronger. Yesterday she successfully twisted a doorknob and Kim clapped. That looks painful, Amanda said. From now on I will see clapping as self-harm.

Kim's counterfeit Amandas fill the page, a blank sky of delirious hard-winged birds.

–Angle it more the other way. The D.

Two years ago, Amanda spent weeks choosing the tile for the small kitchen. She told Kim about Italian mosaics — that what makes them look perfect was the off-kilter pieces concealed in the design, the pieces that set the whole thing moving. Kim said, It's a floor. Amanda said, Tiles are important. Choice by choice by choice every small thing is important.

–No the S should be swoopier, Amanda says.

–Like this?

–No no no that looks like a worm. The S is supposed to create the momentum for the rest of my last name.

–I just write my name in cursive.

–You don't really have a signature, though.

–What about this one?

–Maybe if you did it faster.

–I'm going as fast as I can.

–Don't think about it.

–But I'm learning it.

Amanda smiles and Kim thinks, angrily: I sound like one of her students. Kim has listened to Amanda complain bitterly about "collaborative pedagogy," about how the worst collaborator on the planet is an upper-middle-class eight-year-old male. Her girls are eager to please, little soldiers chanting optimistic mantras. Hello Kitty informants.

Kim slams the pen down.

Picks it up again, slower.

She writes Amanda's name.

–That's it. Almost. Make it more like me.

More like her. If Amanda were injured permanently, Kim thinks, how many things could she learn to do for her, how many things would she have to do for her? Could she become a shadow Amanda, a second Amanda composed only of skills, tasks? The signatures pile up. If Amanda died, how long could Kim pretend she was alive by imitating her signature? Everything comes to their house. Bank statements, the pension statement, the credit card bills, dentist bills.

It's only a broken wrist, Kim thinks. This will be over, soon.

Amanda studies the last fake signature, closes one eye, and turns it upside down.

Kim does not ask why she is doing this.

–I'm going to call the hospital about the x-ray they took, Amanda says.

–The x-ray? Why?

–I want a copy. It's my property.

–Your property?

–It's a picture of my body. Of course it's my property.

The x-ray sits secluded on a bright perch in Kim's mind.

Healthy bones, the doctor had said, looking at Kim, and Kim had known that the doctor knew how afraid she was and that the doctor did not respect that fear. The doctor had seen so much more that was so much worse. The doctor had been able to see that. The weaker partner, the partner who drinks in the worry.

Amanda tries to write her signature once for Kim with her right hand. The pen slides from her swollen fingers.

–I can't even write my own name, Amanda says. She folds her head behind her elbows and relinquishes slow sobs into the wood.

–I'll do it. I can do everything.

–No. I need to.

–Amanda.

Footsteps on the stairs. Furious rush of water in the bathroom.

The sounds of Amanda going to bed: the fingersnap of the light switch, the mattress. A heavy stillness.

Kim rarely needs to sign her name for her barista gig at Starbucks and her cashier job at a local bookstore — jobs she had believed to be transitional and then had settled into, surprised by how easy it was to agree to a working rhythm, her days book-ended by Amanda.

She stays at the table for another hour, then another. Her hand moves through the routine of Amanda's name. Again, again, until Amanda's signature is a picture, a series of lines that could mean anything. A bird limping through mid-flight, a lopsided house, half of a face.


**SHOWERING**

–Would you do my back? Can't do it with my left hand.

Kim slides the bar of soap around Amanda's back. The freckle-lines curve out, darken into patches at the base of her neck, an ultrasound of her denser areas. Amanda's shoulders are broader than most women's. Linebacker shoulders, she jokes. Her shoulders drop, shift forward, as Kim pushes the soap against muscles that give way to bone.

–Oh that feels so good.

Amanda leans into the tile wall, her body goes still.

Water scatters off the garbage bag Kim tied around the cast

and sealed with elastics. Moistness wants to get between the skin and the gauze and make a hot itchy home; make Amanda's skin feel like it's peeling off under the plaster. Kim spent an evening reading online about people blowing warm air up under their casts with hair dryers to create brief comfort.

–I'm worried about the cast coming off.

–Why? Won't you be relieved to do stuff again?

–What if it isn't healed?

Amanda's voice is quiet, barely audible over the shower.

–The doctor said it looked fine.

–But they won't really know, until they take the cast off.

Then why think about it, Kim wants to say. But this would sink Amanda into one of her silences. Best not to push it, to let Amanda hang below the surface. Last Christmas, Amanda received an envelope from Toronto. Kim read the address. A woman's name. Gabrielle. A former lover? After Amanda took the envelope away she admitted no, Gabrielle is her sister. She sells insurance. She let Kim ask a few more questions before getting up to clear the dishes, her wrists moving in sharp gestures that meant the conversation was over. Yes, they look similar. Both with dark hair, the same wide nose, the same green eyes, the same pale skin. It's the Irish side of the family. No, Gabrielle didn't go to university. Amanda's the only one who went to university, separated out by awareness, painted out of the picture by education, and then she moved West, moved as far away as possible. Yes, Gabrielle still talks to their parents. Why wouldn't she? The envelope disappeared.

Kim leans in and the water and Amanda's body move away from her in unison.

The soap rides the curves of Amanda's waist, the small of

her back. She turns. Her breasts. The scar on her stomach: an operation from when she was a child. The skin glistens where it healed. The interior of a shell. Who were the people who took her to the hospital, Kim wonders. Was her father tall, short? Was her mother as cold as Amanda has occasionally hinted, after three glasses of wine? Were they simply indifferent, shepherding a daughter through a passing illness? Kim wants to ask what that illness was. Appendicitis, she thinks. It could be something more serious, and she will never know. Medical history she should know, she thinks, putting the soap in the basket that hangs from the curtain rod. If the scar were not there for her to inspect and wash, she would not know how to live while not knowing.

There was a time in Amanda's life when she never felt safe. After she left her hometown and moved here. Just a job and she knew no one. She rented a basement suite. She changed the locks three times in the first season. Rain in the drainpipe sounded like fingers drumming the hollow-core door. Her telephone did not ring for two months. Then the one-year program to be a teacher. You have no idea how good it felt, she told Kim. To know I could live without needing anyone else. You don't know shit until you have to support yourself.

–Black ice, Kim murmurs. Could happen to anyone.

–It's just, it's my right hand.

The water stops.

Kim pulls the elastic off, rolls the plastic bag carefully so that none of the water runs back onto the cast, lifts Amanda's arms to dry her sides, the parts of her body where her skin is the most pale.

## OPENING A CHILDPROOF PILL BOTTLE

The cast has been changed. A new, lightweight cast. This cast is neon green, the colour of Go, the colour of IKEA children's furnishings, the colour of wet new life.

–The colour of the green fuse that drives the fucking whatever, Amanda says.

–Slings and arrows of outrageous etcetera, Kim says.

Amanda holds the childproof pill bottle away from her like a grenade.

–Cripple-proof crap, Amanda says. I need my drugs.

–Open it, Amanda says.

–No, Kim says.

–Amanda raises her cast and says, Open the cripple-proof crack bottle.

She walks with her cast straight out like a toy soldier's bayonet.

Kim backs out of the room.

–Where are you going?

The walls smear at the corners of her eyes. Amanda's feet stampeding behind her.

–What are you doing?

It began as a joke but now Kim doesn't want to stop running.

In the bedroom, she vaults across the bed, lands on the other side.

Amanda arrives in the doorway.

–Are you jumping on the bed?

–It was the fastest way to get over here, Kim says.

–You just wanted me to chase you, Amanda says.

–No.

–You ran into the bedroom.

–So what.

Kim edges the bed, arms crossed. The first time they had sex, Amanda had said afterwards, Are you going to call me again? If you're not going to call me again, you should just tell me now. Months later, Amanda had told her that all her previous girlfriends had been fair-weather lovers. Fair-weather friend, Kim had corrected her. The expression is fair-weather friend. No, Amanda had said. It should be fair-weather lover. Fair-weather lovers are more common. They see more of you, so they know better when to leave. Don't worry, I'm always the one who people leave, Kim had said. That was the beginning.

–Open the bottle, Amanda says.

Kim steps sideways toward one corner of the bed, Amanda skitters toward the other. They edge the other at diagonals. The bed hangs empty between them.

–This isn't funny anymore, Amanda says. Her cast swings, transforms time into ordered anxiety, the flashing green a frantic metronome.

–I can't handle this, Kim says.

–You can't handle this?

–It's too much.

–I'm the one with the broken wrist.

Amanda hurls the bottle onto the middle of the bed.

Pills shake their dry sound up to the empty ceiling.

–You, Amanda says. You are a child.

–No I'm not. I do everything. Everything everything everything.

–So, what? What? You want out?

The pill bottle is unbelievably white, as if polished, the plastic and the label brimming, as if the bottle will burst if she stares at it longer. Kim's eyes shiver and sting. Someone is trying to touch her eyes.

–If you leave me when I'm like this, I will never forgive you.

Kim looks up at her lover. Broad shoulders, the absurd neon-green cast, face painted a red that means no air, that means terror. When Amanda had called the hospital to get the x-ray, the receptionist told her the x-ray was not in its file, was missing. Oh I'm sorry, Kim had said when Amanda had complained in the kitchen — the medical system, how they had lost the evidence of her injury. Then Kim had climbed the stairs, locked the bedroom door and knelt and taken the lucid image of Amanda's bones from the bottom drawer of the bureau. It had been easy to slip in and out of the consultation room on the way back from the washroom that night at the emergency room. She studied the high-contrast portrait. The fissure that had caused all of this was barely visible — a scratch on ice. Her eyes searched for the place of breaking in the grey. The hand is not a solid thing but a cluster of lopsided moons; the fingers drifted off through separations made of nothing solid or available to the light. Muscle and empty blood between the radiant pattern of bone. Why does she stay. Kim placed her finger on the broken line inside Amanda.

–I'm not leaving.

As Kim leans to take the bottle from the middle of the bed, she hears Amanda's footsteps, feels Amanda's arms on her shoulders, then Amanda's chest against her back. Then Amanda's thumbs along the insides of her shoulder blades. Amanda's uninjured hand tracing a straight line down the middle of her back, an old signal of beginning. Amanda's cast scrapes Kim's cheek, pull of her breath. The cast drags across Kim's back. The cast's roughness and warmth.

Breath.

– Open.

## LIFTING HEAVY THINGS

The laundry basket every Sunday, bright wicker, the size of a rain barrel. The cast iron pan, its one handle that gets hot as a poker and sticks out from the stove like a weapon. The compost bucket on the rain-slick porch. The two-litre milk, until they've drunk enough of it. Furniture that seems slightly crooked. Amanda's briefcase after a weekend of marking book reports. The kettle, scattering sparks of water. The sack of bulk brown basmati. Amanda avoids buying dairy, canned soup, frozen dinners that hang from her one good wrist like a sack of river rocks. Kim cooks meals full of light things. Bell peppers, couscous, spices, fresh sausages, greens, nothing with bones. Omelettes fat with beaten whites. She brings home bags of heavy things. Short ribs and cans of hominy, sweet potatoes and a whole small chicken. She labours over the pans and pots of comfort foods, thick juices and meat browned and stewed. She cuts rosemary and bay leaves from the plants not strangled by the hard winter's frost, she arranges her offerings. She needs two hands to lift the cast iron pan with the chicken at its centre from the oven. Kim carves the heavy knife through the chicken's skin. Kim lifts the new potatoes rolled in blackened rosemary and oil travelling like mercury on the base of the pan. Kim carries the plates to the table, Kim strikes the match for the candles, holding the box with its rough strip with her left hand, flicking the match with her right. Kim lifts the heavy things, all the things to be washed and emptied and changed. She lifts the weeks that follow, when Amanda's hand re-emerges from the neon chrysalis. The wrist pale and soft like a newborn thing. The hand a clumsy human hook. She lifts it. She lifts all of Amanda's furious half-strength in her two good hands.

# THE
# BODIES
# OF
# OTHERS

**THE CHALK** in Sasha's fingers paints onto the board with waxy clarity. She's giving a presentation about semicolons. Making the letters into perfect shapes, she copies out the examples she planned last night in her father's apartment. When she finishes, Carolyn Tsang raises her hand.

"But what do semicolons really *mean*?" Carolyn Tsang says.

Sasha stares at her, feels her balance fade. The laughter of her classmates swells as she turns, raises her chalk, and writes her answer. Unease shuffles up and down the rows.

:        ;

YOU    ME

Scattered giggles, one guffaw, and then the sound of wind against the windows.

"Sasha, would you like to tell us about what you've written?" the teacher asks. Sasha shakes her head, no, and walks back to her desk.

Later, in the schoolyard, Sasha stares into Carolyn Tsang's face. Around them there is the schoolyard's dust-cheeked action. Kids flow past and jump back with the sounds of hooked fish being wrenched out of water. This is the fifteen-minute safety zone after school when the borders dissolve between kids from the houses up the hill close to the university and the kids from down here, from the city's old homes wrapped in the tangled roots of native gardens. Sasha stands stiff and still, staring into Carolyn Tsang's face because Carolyn Tsang's words make Sasha's world.

"I really liked your presentation today," Carolyn Tsang says.

One minute the schoolyard is full and the next it is deserted as kids drop like leaves through the autumn air and blow into the minivans that vanish them up the road.

Carolyn Tsang stares at Sasha with an intense curiosity. It is Carolyn Tsang whom Sasha holds responsible for her position at this school — Carolyn Tsang who ensures that Sasha lives by her sentences, uncertain stretches of words that Sasha balances along, picking her way forward, stepping and skidding, always feeling a few words in front of her for the rotted parts that will plunge her under. She cannot remember when it started, because it has always been this way.

So why is Carolyn Tsang standing here now, speaking to her? Suddenly, they are walking together across the grass away from the school. Carolyn Tsang flounces her black hair with the self-assurance of a seventh grader.

"Where're we going?"

"To my place. Where else?" She is going to Carolyn Tsang's house. Right now. She is. "Where do *you* live?"

"Oh. Um. East. With my mom. And with my dad sometimes. He lives downtown in an apartment. But only for weekends and stuff?"

"So they're divorced?"

"Yeah."

"Sucks to be you!" Carolyn Tsang tilts her face upward and releases laughter like sharp-winged silver birds that fill the sky. "My parents would never split up," she says. "Chinese."

They walk quickly, looking straight ahead, until they stop in front of a large Vancouver Special: a beige box like thousands of others in the city, grey waves of rained-down grit rippling the stucco like eye makeup running on pale skin.

"This is it."

The entranceway smells of new leather. In the kitchen, Carolyn Tsang speaks to an old woman in a language Sasha doesn't understand. The woman looks appraisingly at Sasha, who stands quietly, hands pocketed. Then they hurry out of the kitchen and into a bedroom, small and sweet-smelling.

"Sit."

Sasha sits on the edge of the bed and Carolyn Tsang stands at the bookcase with her back to her and runs her fingers across the spines of novels. For several minutes she takes books out and slides them back in. Then, quickly, she turns to Sasha.

"So what do you want to do?"

"I dunno. What'd you have me over for?"

"Whatever. You *followed* me here."

"No I didn't."

The room is silent and still. Sasha picks up her backpack, thumps down the stairs to the door, and leaves. Vancouver rain falls, blisters her skin.


A week later, Carolyn Tsang asks Sasha to be her partner for art period and Sasha accepts. The assignment is to trace their bodies onto large pieces of paper. The class files out to the basketball court and spreads their sheets over the pavement.

Since the semicolon day, Carolyn Tsang has changed. She catches up to Sasha in the hall on the way to gym class. She turns and smiles at Sasha when something funny happens in class. The other girls in the class aren't happy with the change — their former leader favouring the one they previously ignored, flamboyantly, meaningfully. Sasha can feel their stares. The skin of Carolyn Tsang's face is pulled tight, like delicate paper a flung pebble could tear through.

The teacher speaks over them as she distributes the markers. After the outlining is done they will fill in details to make the pictures *authentic*. Really try to *personalize* them, she says. Then the drawings will be so real they will be able to practically get up and walk around. Sasha pictures an empty court milling with simple, paper people. This is a world in which she might be able to safely live, she thinks.

Carolyn Tsang lies down on the paper. Legs apart, arms out, her body spare in dark Gap jeans and hoodie, eyes shut.

Sasha moves above her, barely breathing. She holds herself up with one arm and with the other hand she drags the marker along the sides and insides of Carolyn Tsang's legs and up around her torso and head in one long stroke. In order to move this way Sasha must move neither toward nor away, remain outside of falling or pulling. She slips once and brushes Carolyn Tsang's forehead — her whole body flinches like a wing. Then the return to stillness, the perfect suspension of an underwater thing. Carolyn Tsang's body directly below hers. The heat of her face. The heat of her face. Sasha slows the travel of her hand that holds the marker. She could continue to trace and retrace her body indefinitely, she thinks, making the line thicker and darker until the line was as thick as the form it contains. She could continue to draw Carolyn Tsang's body until the drawing could stand up and walk around.

The teacher walks past and Sasha lifts upward, flushed.

"Done."

Carolyn and Laura kneel and fill in the paper girl's eyes, mouth, nose, and ears and argue over how to commit her shoes to paper.

"Don't draw them straight," Carolyn Tsang says. "I'll look like a duck. Don't make me look like a duck." Then she says, "Lie down, it's your turn."

The body above Sasha hovers. The felt tip squeals and Carolyn Tsang is drawing her. Sasha feels what she has never felt before — the feeling of a body very close to hers, inside the boundaries she has been taught to maintain between her body and the bodies of others. The presence smells of grass and sweat. Both scents faint, the breath of plants. The breath repeats, repeats, as Sasha is committed to paper. The cold of the cement strobes through her as the warmth above moves lower. The hand brushes her shoulders, climbs and circles her head, her hair is brushed again with the side of a skin not cold like cement or empty as air, but warm with a warmth that carries with it echo under Sasha's skin, a fleeting heat that the girl under her takes, the her who is not her. This time, when it is done, Sasha lies with her eyes held shut.

"I'm done," says a voice exactly like Carolyn Tsang's.

The court is gone from under her body. She hears distant noises.

"Sasha?" A taller voice. Farther, then close to her skin. "Sasha?"

Now a chorus, a group of voices calling her. Some worried, some jeering.

"Sasha? Sasha?"

She cannot be called out.


The paper girls hang on the classroom wall. Side by side, expression unchanging. Sasha gazes into their white faces, at the thick marker encircling their eyes.

The word is out. Sasha sits still at her desk and knows that it is there — something curled inside her desk, something savage inside that mess, waiting. You win, she wants to lift the top of her desk and tell it — you win you win you win. Her desk is one in the classroom's tight array, their bases bolted to the linoleum. The geometry of desks decides the arrangement of cliques, the currents of power that flow through the room and split at the deviant terms. Words cut around her, strand her inside a dry triangle of silence. The message is passed like a hot stone from hand to hand around the room. Sasha looks up at the paper girls and waits, looks proud. Her pride is a built-up nothing, her last chance.

Sasha was young when she began to live in multiple worlds. She was seven, when her parents split up. From their house in Kitsilano her father moved into an apartment downtown where she visits some weekends. A few blocks away from his apartment there's a Denny's that fills with drag queens late at night, emptying plates of fries and chicken strips. As a treat he once took her there for a milkshake at one in the morning and she marvelled at their big hair and confusing extraordinary faces as he rushed her past. That year, the way she began to see her classmates. As playmates, not as people to be taken seriously. When they spoke she was not curious. The eager ones made her sad. She had learned to move between neighbourhoods, had seen that worlds are made up of different walks, different jackets, different ways of speaking. Her classmates still do not know this and she will never explain it to them. They do not know that a change of self, a choice of self, is possible, or that it exists at all. This knowledge, her sharp treasure. Words, grand cards in a constant bluff.

Lunchtime!

Binders and books slap into piles. Sasha and her classmates push down the hallway toward the gym where everyone eats at long tables before the fresh prismatic yes of the outside, the high dance of the swings, the tetherball post to lean against, performing disinterest.

Sasha's day is broken down into strategies, not actions. She must approach it as a puzzle and then it is tolerable, there is a way to get through. The figuring-out and figuring-through that is survival. It begins with her arrival in the morning. Which entrance of the school to go into. All the primary-colour doors clotted with kids — every entrance a region of water with complicated tides. She must know where the fast currents are, the turns and undertows, where to expect the firm ankle-grab that drags her under. She must know well the sinkholes with wet words swirling down. Above all, she must recognize the constant possibility of drowning. There is no map for this. There is nowhere to leave signs to hold on to. Don't hit. No lying. Be nice. A sign, a hold, is a drop of ink into the map that slides, a newt or a black tear. A frantic word sinking into a book of sand. Rules that sink, drift.

Sasha's stomach fills when she enters the gym and sees the only empty seat — directly across from Carolyn Tsang. She arranges all the parts of her lunch on the table in front of her before she lifts her head.

"We all know what you did," Carolyn Tsang says. Sasha stares back at her. There is no strategy for this. Only a wandering, a terror. "And I just want to say to you that it was very inappropriate."

"I don't know what you're talking about."

"You know what I'm talking about."

"No I don't."

"Yes you do."

"Well why don't you explain it to me then?"

Sasha wonders what changed and why whatever it was has now changed back. There was an ease that seems impossible to regain, a warm wind through which she fell and fell without fear. She remembers sitting in the quiet of Carolyn Tsang's room on the semicolon day and the silence as Carolyn Tsang sorted through her bookcase with her back to Sasha. She wonders if it would be strategic to mention that now.

"When you were drawing me — you were so *close,*" Carolyn Tsang says.

The girls around the table turn. They enjoy acting so old, having this chance to show what they can do. Sasha looks around and none of these girls is made of paper. They are all skin and bones and weight and there is danger.

"That was the assignment."

"Whatever. You're a freak."

Sasha gets up and walks toward the door to the schoolyard. By the time she reaches the door, she is running.

"Hey! Hey!"

Students straggling into the yard congregate, sensing a fight.

"Hey!"

"What?"

"You know what happened."

"No, I don't."

Carolyn Tsang paces forward until she stands in front of Sasha. Once again, Sasha feels the other girl's breath on her skin, but now it is cold — puffs of October air that feel like false punches glancing gently off her cheeks.

"Say what you did."

"What are you talking about?"

"Say it!"

"Back off."

A murmur of agreement fattens the crowd. Sasha hears it. She could still get out of this.

"Say it!"

"I said back off."

"Say it!"

Carolyn Tsang reaches forward and grabs her wrist.

"You kissed me! You kissed me!"

The crowd's murmur swells in volume, fades and migrates like drumbeats. As Sasha turns away, Carolyn Tsang puts out an arm to keep her, and Sasha runs into it, sends Carolyn Tsang spinning into the dirt. Carolyn Tsang lies there, crying loudly. The crowd begins to break apart. A teacher rushes across the yard and pulls Sasha away while another teacher kneels beside Carolyn Tsang and hurries her off toward the school. Sasha watches her leave, her stomach an ache. The teacher places one arm across her shoulders, as if to push her forward. He teaches one of the older grades, has never spoken to Sasha before. "Deep breaths, let's get going," he mutters.

The sensation of Carolyn Tsang falling refuses to leave Sasha's arm. The fall so easy, the fall of a small thing. The memory appears in bright shades of blue, a night a few months before she and her mother left their old house in Kitsilano. Her parents arguing at the kitchen counter, her father turning too fast as her mother tried to pass him. Her forehead glancing off the counter's edge. Red arrow edging downwards. She staggered into the hallway and blood flowed onto the carpet where her head landed, the shadow of her father sprinting to snatch dishrag off the oven door. That blood stayed in the carpet no matter how much her father scrubbed it when he prepared the house to be sold months later. Sasha watched this around the edge of the doorway and then ran to her bedroom, lay in bed.

At two in the morning when she sat up, she believed that

her mother was dead. Her feet carried her down the hall to the door of her parents' bedroom. Two fingers light as insects on the knob and it swung inwards. Inside, they were curled together in bed, moving slowly against each other. Breaths crackled and whistled. The light in the room blue and round over them in one wide wave. The black bed and transparent ceiling. Sasha stepped back from the door, struggling to emerge from the water in which she found herself. She sank slowly to the bottom without thinking about water. Inside the water only thoughts of air are possible. At the bottom of the water there is still farther to go.

The next day in the schoolyard they are waiting.

"Fight fight fight," they chant. "*Fight fight fight.*"

An army melts and regroups, lunges through dust. Sasha looks up and there are more of them but still none of them.

Hey hey get her get her. Hey hey hey get her!

For an uncombed instant she is running, body shoeless, arms to the sky, free from the backdrag of words and fists. Then the ground shoves its flat hands up.

"What is this? What is this?" The teacher's voice is from a Charlie Brown cartoon — *whu whu whu, whu whu whu*. Sasha shuts her eyes and is on the basketball court, sinking into that stillness, its safest place. "Well? What is this?" the teacher demands of the attackers, the line-up of Nike barbarians, their rainbow of brightly coloured backpacks in a pile a safe distance away, their faces lowered.

The dust has settled, erasing the sudden violent world. Sasha waits, covered in dust.

The same teacher from yesterday, but today his body moves quickly, bearing down on her fast, and his two strong hands pull her up. The teacher walks with his head down, his hand in hers. By the time they reach the office Sasha is trotting to keep up. He notices, slows, and pulls her briefly against his side which is warm and smells of chalk. In the nurse's office, she sits on the bench and he kneels, cleans her cuts with a clear liquid that burns. Her eyes hunt his careful fingertips.

"So tell me about what happened."

"I stole one of their Discmans."

"Oh? Whose?"

"Carolyn Tsang."

He nods slowly.

"You don't have one?"

"No."

"Do you like music?"

"Yeah."

"What kind of music do you like?"

"Different kinds."

"Did you get a chance to listen to the Discman, even?"

"Yeah, a bit."

"What kind of music was it?"

She hesitates, realizes her mistake. He will find Carolyn Tsang and ask her what CD was in her Discman. Carolyn Tsang will tell him that her mother won't let her have one. Sasha has heard her complain about her mother, call her Traditional, which Carolyn Tsang changes into Tradition-anal.

"No. It was Mike's Discman."

"Mike?"

"Mike, Mike. You know. Mike." She takes her arm away.

"What's Mike's last name."

"Mike. He's, I dunno. A couple years younger than me? What. Are you stupid or something?" She wipes the swelling prong of blood under her nose.

"There's no reason to protect them," he says. He avoids looking at her.

"I don't know what you're talking about."

The secretary calls Sasha's mother. The teacher looks out the window at the vans full of kids going past and Sasha feels sorry for him. But it's for his own good. When you're sure to lose, it's better to know what you're up against. There is nothing he could do to help, even begin to unwind it, the everything of it, back to its beginning, far before the kiss. She cannot remember a beginning, because it has always been this way. The scramble of the attack begins to fade behind the steady pulse of her blood and she pulls her knees up, puts her head down, folds her arms between her kneecaps and temples, letting her breaths, each one like a resounding echo bouncing back to her from the other side, slow her body, bring her down to this. *Fight fight fight.*

Sasha moves quickly across the dark schoolyard, the moon cool and bright. She edges the school, staying inside its inked shadow, avoiding the sound-trap of gravel. She climbs the fire-escape ladder, setting each foot firmly to silence the shaky metal frame. She transfers her backpack to the front of her body, swings on to the shallow ledge that runs the length of the building, and starts to edge her way across the outside of the school. At the fifth window, she opens her backpack, takes out her mother's hammer, and gives it one fast swing in the centre of the window. Glass sprays into the classroom and across her shoes, shards spinning off the ledge and out into the darkness. She works outward from the hole, shuffling her feet to avoid the spray of glass. She crouches and swings one leg inside, falls hard onto the floor.

She moves quickly. She drags a desk to the back wall, balances on its surface and pulls down all the paper children within her reach, then shifts the desk and pulls down more. She is pulling down the second-last traced, cartoon-featured duplicate of a classmate when she hears the sirens. She searches for Carolyn Tsang's outline and her own and stuffs them into her backpack with as many others as she can fit. She runs.

A few lights snap on around the field, houses awakened by the sirens. Sasha slides rapidly along the ledge, the sirens wailing out front, distant flat sounds of car doors slamming.

She nearly slips swinging down onto the ladder, her fingers and shoes slipping down the rungs, the work of climbing down getting in the way of falling down. Pavement shocks her legs, her feet fly out under her, running. She rounds the corner of the first portable, slips through its shadow, weaves across the parking lot, ducking under the curved profiles of the few cars left overnight. The sirens have stopped. She looks over her shoulder as she bursts finally onto the sidewalk and down the road. Every light in the school has been turned on. The building looks as if it is ablaze.

# WIRE
# BOY

**WE ARRIVE** at my grandmother's house and my mother stops
me again outside the door, holds my shoulder and says to me,
"Remember what we talked about. No funny business." My father looks at me over his shoulder and nods. He is much bigger
than I am, as big as some trees. My mother tangles between us,
gets tangled up until she pulls free whatever is in my hands.
Usually it is wire. Almost always it is wire. Tonight she made
me promise to stay away from it. No funny business in front

of the relatives. But everybody already knows anyway. And I am so young for this. Only seven yet. With George it started much later. I'm not supposed to talk tonight either. It's not normal for little boys to talk the way I do. But most of all nothing with the wire. My father rings the doorbell. "Remember, you," my mother says. "I'll let you play with your box when we get home." I nod but I know that we will be here all evening and into the night too once the drinking starts and my father will carry me sleeping out to the backseat of the car and I know I won't be able to resist for that long.

My grandmother opens the door, holds me tightly until my mother pulls me away. She knows I get overwhelmed. It is hard for me to be held, another reason that I am strange.

I run past them into the living room full of uncles and cousins. My father is by the fire with my grandfather drinking already. My cousins surround me and talk about what they're getting for Christmas tomorrow morning. My turn to tell about gifts. I make things up. A baseball bat. Comic books. Even while I say these things they sound boring. There is only one thing I want. There is only one thing. My parents will give it to me in a wrapped box tomorrow morning under the tree covered with the handmade decorations my mother collects. No lights on the tree this year. I can't resist pulling them down.

I look away from my cousins talking about what we're eating later, the food my aunts and grandmother have been cooking all day. Four different kinds of pie, they say, and then chant, four different kinds, four different kinds. I see my mother standing on the other side of the room, making sure that I'm keeping my promise. Her eyes follow me carefully. Lately I've started to see that my parents aren't just my parents, that they aren't there only in being there for me. I know this when my mother pulls me away from what I want. The black vines that come out of lamps, that tangle between the TV and the VCR, all the powerful strings that hold everything together, those strings full of something I can't touch but can hear whenever I am near it, like singing, and falls dead when it's cut through. Wire.

I concentrate on my cousins and try hard to care about what they're saying. But already the singing is starting to interfere, to sizzle the edges off everything. For a few seconds I let it pour in. The room is full of it, full of things held together by it. The singing gets louder and louder until it is deafening. I press my hands into my ears and squeeze my eyes shut. My cousins laugh. They love it when I do weird things like this. Then I shut it out. Silence.

"Chris!"

My mother has seen and is running across the room toward me. She pulls me away from my cousins and past the fireplace where the men are beached on barcaloungers, drinking. My father is talking to my grandfather about the price of gas. She pushes me into a tiled room full of noise and things flying around. Two of my mother's sisters stick their fingers into my hair, ears, near my mouth. A pot of gravy is poured into white jugs. Trays of roasted potatoes are lifted from the oven and forked into serving dishes. They've been cooking all day, my mother told me on the way over, her face hanging in the black windshield like a balloon. So you better behave.

An aunt scratches my ribs to make me giggle. Instead I pull away.

"You getting hungry, Chris? Almost ready!"

"No thank you. I'm not hungry," I say.

Laughter fills the kitchen and I feel the heat of the blush on my mother's face several feet above me.

"Not hungry! Don't you want your Christmas Eve dinner?"

"No thank you. I don't really care about Christmas."

The laughter comes again, this time louder. I press my hands over my ears. My mother's hand tightens on my shoulder.

"You got yourself a card there, Anne," an aunt says and my mother laughs a little.

She pulls me back through the door into the living room and falls to one knee so she is the same height as me. Her hands clamp my shoulders tight.

"You behave, hear?" she says soft, urgent.

"I am!"

"Remember our talk from before?"

"Yeah."

"No funny business, Chris, none."

"Okay."

"You will not embarrass me in front of my family. You will not."

"Okay-ay."

"Okay-ay," she mimics and I glare at her, think, let me go, let me go, let me go.

She lets me go and I fly across the room, away from the noise of the kitchen, away from her hundred, snaking constrictions. Around the clutch of cousins. Their shrill voices run together and sound like a beehive.

"Chris!"

An uncle's large hand reaches for me and I swerve around it, continue to run between the legs taller than lamps, bouncing off furniture, off the shine and hot of the fire, until I run out and past the whiteness and long walls and then against a door and hang against it, sweating, breathing, breathing.

I sag into it and it falls away in front of me, like a curtain.

Inside, it swirls around me. My skin gets taut, then shimmers away from my body. I am in a room full of it. A bright face looks at me, a square face crowded with numbers and small pictures. The screen sits on a long table that fills the whole wall. A narrow metal box and a squatter metal box hum on the table. I have seen one of these things in the gas station my father owns, buzzing on his office desk, a yellowed plastic box I can tell he resents from the papers stacked all over it. This one is better than my father's, I can tell. White and smooth as the inside of a Lego rocket. I have never been in this room before and I see that it is full of things that do not fit the other rooms that are pink and brown and full of my grandmother's collections of small ugly things. Now I remember my mother complaining to my father about George. All he does is sit around fiddling with his machines all day, she said. At least he's got something to keep him busy, my father said. George is my mother's youngest brother. She has five brothers, all too big for me to understand or even look at all at once. All of them welders or farmers except for George. George is even bigger than the others, bigger than anyone I've ever seen, but he doesn't seem that big because he's so pale and when he moves it's nervous, so that nothing he touches ever moves. At the big family dinners he sits beside my grandmother, no one talks to him, and if anyone touches him it's careful, like he's a really expensive chair.

I turn and look around the rest of the room. Shelves piled with pieces of metal, screws, springs, plugs, and thick ribbon that shimmers. I turn again and face a coat rack draped in wire. The wire hangs down from the branches of the coat rack and touches the floor.

I walk forward and put my hand flat against the screen and it glows through, webs my fingers with light. It goes all the way through me and out again. I want to reach around and hold onto what is behind. My mother's words stop me. Her words pound and keep on pounding inside me. No Chris, no. When we get home? Maybe. You might get to play with your box when we get home. My box of wire is my best thing. My mother keeps it on a shelf at the top of the closet in the hall. I've wrapped the wire up in balls to look like my mother's balls of yarn. Before my mother made the box of wire they tried to keep me from it for months, keep me from the only thing I want. I watched my father tape up all the plugs in our house and except for school my mother only took me to the park. She doesn't believe me when I tell her I can hear the wire. It has always been there, the sound of it, like singing. A singing that is high and pure. She couldn't keep me from it, so she made the box.

She can't hide all the other things about me though, all the things that won't fit in a box. That I talk too fast, all at once, too much. Too much, Chris, you're always too much. That I start to move and can't stop moving. That I don't care about people much. Worst of all, that I don't care about Christmas.

"But all little boys love Christmas," my mother said.

"I don't. I don't care about Christmas."

I didn't say it to make her mad, just because it's true.

"Yes you do. All little boys do."

"I don't care. I don't want it."

She looked at me like I had taken something away from her, something big. Tonight I have to care about Christmas. And I am not allowed to find any wire. Everywhere I go I find the wire. My parents don't take me to restaurants anymore. I am a public embarrassment. That's what my mother said.

The screen is warm and slippery now under my skin. Eyes shut. The door opens and closes. I turn around fast. My heart won't work because I am afraid. I take my hand off the screen and wipe it off on my jeans.

George almost fills the doorway right up.

"Hi Chris. Dinner's ready," George says.

George has slow eyes. The circles around the black parts are almost the same colour as water. His slow water eyes move from me to the computer to the shelves full of things and back to me again.

"You like my room?" he says.

"No."

"Dinner's ready."

He shuts the door behind him.

My mother will be looking for me. First she will look upstairs in my grandparents' bedroom where they have a big-screen TV, a VCR, and a DVD player all stacked up across from the bed. The last time that's where she found me, kneeling down with my fingers dug deep in the black bundles.

I don't want to leave this room. But they will be looking for me. I go to the coat rack and run my fingers through the long, hanging wires. The wire is like hair and I drag my fingers down through it slowly. It feels good on my skin, smooth and cold and I like how every piece separates out for my fingers to touch. I leave the room.

"Chris!"

My mother is running toward me from the end of the hall-way.

"Where have you been? Everyone's already at the table."

"Nowhere."

She frowns at me, then rubs my hair and pulls one corner of my mouth.

"Come on sweetie. Let's go eat. Christmas dinner!"

Everyone's sitting around the huge table in the dining room. So many heads turn toward us when we walk in.

"Found him!" my mother yells triumphantly and every-body laughs.

I am lifted into a chair in the middle of my cousins. They all seem the same to me. My father calls them the family litter. My father and mother are strange because I don't have any broth-ers or sisters, there's just me. When my grandmother asks my mother if she's got another one coming my mother says back that the one she's got is plenty enough work for her and thank you very much.

My grandmother carries out the turkey as big as George's head and everyone ooohs and aaahs. My aunts and my mother carry out shiny white bowls full of potatoes, yams, stuffing, parsnips, cranberry sauce, biscuits, and then the jugs of gravy.

I don't notice the argument starting because I am concen-trating on how to get pieces of yam, biscuit, and turkey onto my fork all at the same time.

"Tourist prices." My grandfather's voice just above the others and angry.

"Gas is expensive, Earl," my father says.

My father's gas station is on the highway that makes the edge of our town. Just under everything in the town, so quiet, you can always hear the sound of traffic.

"Why should I pay tourist prices? My own son-in-law the owner and I pay tourist prices," my grandfather says.

"Earl. That's enough," my grandmother says and stares at the small glass of whiskey he's snuck in behind her good crystal.

"We get by, Earl. You know we just get by," my father says.

"Only honest way to live is farming and building," my grandfather says. He always says that. "Live on what you make," he says next and lifts his glass toward someone invisible.

"Earl," my grandmother says. "Earl."

"Tourist prices. Tourist prices. Your gas station is making us into a Goddamn road stop. Don't tell me you're not making money. How could that boy be like he is without money in that house?"

"What has Chris got to do with this?" My father's face is twisted now, like bark on a dead tree.

"Indulgence. Indulgence. Indulgence," my grandfather says, and I see some of my uncles and aunts nod.

I ask, "But what about George's special room?"

When the words are in the air in front of me I am surprised to be staring straight into my grandfather's face for the first time. The bones in his cheeks are high and thin like my mother's, but padded with skin that puffs out and is pink and red with flecks of pure white. Blue lines around his eyelids thin as lashes. He's wearing the same thing he always wears, a plaid shirt and a sweater made of something soft and light. He has so many sweaters like this that I hardly ever see him wear the same one twice. When my father talks about my grandfather he always complains about the sweaters. Two hundred bucks a pop for what? The same cashmere thing over and over again. Your father's a crook, Anne, he says. Got rich buying people's land for nothing when they had nothing then selling it off for twenty times the price. When I hear this I don't understand why my grandfather says the things he says about himself. All the things he calls himself. An everyman. A layperson. A man of the land. Same as the next, no different.

The table is a ring of faces turned toward me. Waiting.

"What did you say, boy?" my grandfather says.

"Chris," my father corrects him.

"George's room. His special room."

"What room? George, you have a special room?" an aunt bursts in, turns sweetly to George. "How nice."

"Chris," my mother says. This is another thing wrong with me. I don't know when to be quiet.

"I don't know what room you're talking about," my grandfather says.

"It's a room full of it. Full of it. Full of it. Full of it."

The table is silent. My cousins start to laugh and squirm in their seats. It's fun for them when I'm weird but only when we're playing.

"That boy needs help, Anne. See that he gets it," my grandfather says and rises from the table.

When he leaves the meal is over. Nobody says this but as soon as the door shuts behind him my grandmother and aunts get up and start to take the half-full dishes off the table. My cousins melt from their seats. Then my uncles and father.

I keep eating until my mother takes the plate from under my fork.

"Stop it. Stop eating. Why can't you ever just stop?" she says.

My aunts are blind and deaf, hurrying between the table and the kitchen. George is the only one left at the table besides me.

I look at George and for a moment imagine his large pale eyes opening wide into mine, giving me some clue about how it will be and how I will get through. He does not look at me. I want to ask him about the room. I have thought about there being other people like me but I know there probably aren't but still I think about it. There would be a choir that sounds like the wire. George stares straight ahead, doesn't look at me, stares straight ahead. My grandmother comes in from the kitchen. My mother rushes out, her face red and she's crying.

"Dinner's over, Georgie," my grandmother says.

George doesn't answer.

"Dinner's over, sweetheart."

George shakes his head and points at me.

"Chris is done with his dinner too. See? His plate is gone."

When it hits the table George's fist makes the cutlery jump and clang back onto polished wood. I jump my chair back at the force of it.

"Chris, would you go into the living room? You're upsetting George."

"Sorry George. Sorry sorry George sorry sorry sorry."

My grandmother stares at me and then smiles.

In the living room my cousins lock their shoulders in a circle around the Scrabble board. The circle tightens as I approach. It has finally happened. They have cast me out. My uncles and father are around the fire, my grandfather gone for the night, because of me. Two more logs are shoved in and flames and sparks hurl themselves at the brick walls of the hearth.

The Christmas tree stands in the big window that looks out over the front lawn. I walk toward the tree and stand under it, my hands shoved into my pockets so I won't reach up and touch the wire looped around the branches dangling lights in all different colours, begging for my fingers to reach upwards and touch.

My father's voice drifts toward me from the fire a few feet away.

"From the university, yeah. Dunno what for. They're interested in this wire stuff. He wants an electric set for Christmas now. God knows what we're gonna do about that. I think Anne got him some socks and books. Doesn't seem right to get him the set. Might make him worse. You saw him at dinner. Anne's at her wit's end. She has to be watching him all the time or he gets into everything. We went to White Spot for Sunday dinner last month and he up and crawled under the table and took apart the plug in the wall down there and part of the floor lamp. You should have seen it. He gutted the damn thing. Pulled out all the wires. Asked him why and he said he was improving it. Anne and I were wondering why he was being so quiet under there. She's afraid he'll turn out the same as George see. Sometimes I think she's right. Hate to think that way about my own boy though. Chris's strange and all. I'm the first to admit it but he's not a, you know. A retard."

They didn't tell me what the tests I wrote at school were for until two men came to interview me because of them. The teacher told me they were from the biggest university in the province and wanted to talk to me because I'd done really well on the tests. They'd already talked to my mother. They asked me to spell my last name and I did it for them four times to make sure they got it exactly right.

"T-O-E-W-S-T-O-E-W-S-T-O-E-W-S-T-O-E-W-S."

One of them started taking notes after I did that.

"How long have you been hearing wire, Christopher?"

"I do. I do hear wire."

"That's fine, Christopher. Just tell us how long this has been happening."

"Since forever."

"What does it feel like when it's happening?"

They wore dark blue pants with dark blue jackets that matched and one of them wrote down everything I said but I told them anyways because it might be the only time anyone ever asks me that. I pointed to where all the wire was in the walls in the room we were sitting in. I told them how I can't go anywhere without knowing where all the wire is and wanting to find it. How I understand wire-talk better than I understand people-talk. How it sounds like singing. How wire-talk is quick quick quick like that and always has a thing to do, a light to light, a car to start up, something to start up or burn up. How my mother tried to make me stop and told me that if I ignored it, it would go away. How it didn't go away because it is a thing inside of me and I don't want it to either.

The living room is hot and late, the fire bobs down then is scooped up again in sparks and poured on to more hungry wood. My cousins clear the Scrabble board, all the tiny wooden tiles go clack clack clack as they fall like water. I stand by the tree and nobody looks at me. I look around to make sure my mother is still in the kitchen. Then I leave.

My grandparents's house is big and full of doors. I open and close doors. How did I find it last time? The back of my neck starts to sting with panic. Finally I stop and listen and find the room at the end of a side hall.

This time the room is dark when I enter. Someone has turned everything off. My hand goes to the light switch. On. Off. On off. On off.

The screen is just glass now, cool and dead. I press a button and it flashes once and starts to buzz. I press another button and one of the metal boxes starts to throb. The room is quiet except for the sound of these things. Far away I hear the arguing of my cousins, the rumble of the men, the clanking of the kitchen. I will not be missed for more than ten minutes and this time they will know where to find me.

My mother will come. She will look at me, disappointed. She will not say what I know she doesn't say only so that she doesn't have to hear the words. "You're just like George." But I'm not like George. His stare back at me at the table when he finally turned his head as I left was not even tired.

I want to stay in this room. I don't want to be found or even to go home.

The coat rack draped with wires is in the corner and I go to it. The long looped ends touch the floor, creating a thick curtain, hang heavy in my hands, slip against my wrists. I crawl into the empty protected space in the middle of the curtains and the wires start to slide off the arms of the coat rack, slide down towards me.

The wire is all different colours. Red black green white blue and silver and gold. I crouch down and put one arm up over me and then it all comes down and I let it. I pull and wind it all around me until it covers my body completely, I am hidden inside a nest of it.

I wrap my arms and legs around me and the wire is just more arms, more legs. I crouch, covered and hidden, waiting. They will never find me here.

# PRESERVATION

**THEY WOULD KILL US** if they knew what we do here, in the turtle pit. Her hands clench behind my neck like a second bundle of optic nerves, giving my eyes the strength to withstand the intense glare of this place — black rock walls, washed-out sky. Above the turtle pit, the fields sweep out for gold miles all the way to the town where everyone lives. We crawl under the truck. Its shadow is the only escape from the heat. Underneath, it smells of oil, dust, and our sweat. All the fossils in the turtle pit lie in heaps around us. The sharp mouths of rocks bruise us as we roll and our cries echo back for millions of years.

Once, after we make love, she reaches across my body and takes a trilobite from beside my shoulder. She holds it over us — a small prehistoric creature, its back patterned like a brain. I run my finger along the black contours of its form, then around the lines of her body. We scramble into the hot light and pull our clothes over our bodies. I jump into my jeans. She buttons up the long skirt that she has to wear, even in summer. She slides the trilobite into my pocket where it bulges beside my wallet.

"Wait, wait," I say and rummage in the truck for my camera.

"No, no," she protests, smiling, then afraid.

"Just stand there."

This is the image of her that I will keep. Arms akimbo, her wild smile, like a kid posing with Mickey Mouse at Disneyland, one of the turtles at her side. The black shape absorbs all light, bends all space toward it. Then, a long sequence of her standing at mock attention, hands linked around her slim stomach. As I click the shutter again, again, she stares solemnly into the camera's small eye, the fossilized turtle resting at her side. Then she bends and kisses its blunt black top, hard, falls to her knees with her arms around it. My laughter bounces and shines off the rock walls.


My dad and my stepmom Anne named it the turtle pit. The pit was dug out by a logging company to get rock to grind up for roads, then abandoned. The walls are loaded with fossils — once, it must have been a riverbed or cove, protected and fertile. My dad found the turtle pit on the way back from a camping trip. He took Anne, an amateur fossil nut, then me. We stared at the turtles coming out of the earth like tumours or diamonds. I ran my fingers over them, feeling something garish and magical in me.

A few months later, they drove out there in the truck of a friend who works in construction and used his equipment to lift two of the turtles into the back of the truck. They set one turtle down on either side of the door to our house. Door ornaments, or prehistoric sentinels. A real hoot, they said. Walking between them for the first time, I couldn't help but feel judged by the ages. The week before, I had met her.

It was my idea for us to start going to the turtle pit. It was just two hours out of town and at the end of its own abandoned road. In the back of my mind, I was reassured that a place made of rock couldn't keep a record. All soft surfaces could betray us with the marks of our bodies.

Every afternoon after we made love for those first few weeks in her house, we stood in the laundry room while the washing machine churned the sheets clean. It was our ritual. Hip against tilted hip; breast against breast; the white metal edge of the machine against her back or mine. The basement room barely lit by the sun that worked its way through the ground-level window. We listened for her father's footsteps above us. Once, I had to scramble out the window and crawl along the side of the house to walk the mile to where I had parked my truck.

It was only a matter of time before someone walked into the empty house when her bedroom was live with the sounds of us.

"It'll be safe there," I told her. I drove her past our house quickly, once, and she craned her neck to see the turtles by the door. My stepmom Anne waved at my truck from the front window.

We've been coming here ever since, for months now, to the turtle pit. One narrow road leads down into it. The tire marks from my truck wrinkle the dust. After every visit, I walk up and down, checking for others, then kneel and wipe ours away.

All the houses on our side of town are full of stuff found on the beaches — foam buoys the weight of volcanic rock, smoothed glass, and shells printed with galaxies. Glass floats, beautiful as bathyspheres, picked from kelp beds. Cans of pop that drifted, unopened, all the way from China. Someday a researcher will go around and collect all this stuff, put it together, and write a true report about everyone who lives here.

An archaeologist. That's what I'm going to be. I can dig through and pull out what matters, I tell her. I have a way with layers. She laughs, pulls the back of her hand across my cheek, then holds it around my breast. "Sure you are," she says. The piping of the truck's belly shines above her like the dark network of a body. She hates making love in front of the turtles. "I feel like they're watching us," she whispers.

In her part of town, decorations harvested from beaches are absent from porches and mantles. Wooden houses like cabins stand side by side, cut from the same tube of frozen cinnamon-coloured cookie dough. We met at the Hallowe'en dance at the skating rink — the only chance for kids from the high school and the Traditional school, the thumper school, to meet. The ice had been melted off for repairs, revealing a dance floor of concrete that was unbelievably smooth. She stood with the girls from the thumper school. They looked like the backup singers for a kitschy German band. They bent down and held their noses above the skin of the punch, suspecting liquor.

I watched her walk onto the dance floor. Her movements to the song were all off. Anyone could tell that she had never danced before. Her legs bowed and swayed under her long skirt. I began to measure time by the movements of her body, not the beats in the music. People stood in a circle around her. The thumper kids backed up. She danced until a tall boy about my age strode forward and stilled her with a finger on her elbow. Oh God, I thought. Not this. Not her.

I can smell my dad from the front door. He sits in the underwater light of the living room, feet up, his fingers around his bottle like a cradle of dirty white rope.

"What're you doin' now?" he says. I hear it wrong, as, "What're you gonna do?" because it's all I think about — when I will leave town, and how I can take her with me. I can't stay around here wearing jeans and driving a truck after graduation. No woman can do that, here.

"I'm going to be an archaeologist," I say.

"Sure you are," he says, his eyes fixed on Dr. Phil. "Ark-ee-oil-oe-jist. Last job I did was cleaning out someone's basement. The pipes were broke. Not the water pipes. The shit pipes. That's a bad job to have. Shovelling out a basement of half-frozen shit. I pretended it was cookie dough." He drains the rest of his beer. "Isn't that what an ark-ee-oil-oe-jist does, though? Digs through everybody else's shit."

I have been reading about fossils in the magazine Anne subscribes to. Fossil comes from the Latin *fossus*, meaning "having been dug up." A living fossil is an informal term — a living species that's a lot like a species that is now living. A trace fossil is activity left in the rock. A fossil isn't something that worked to get that way. All it takes is the right place, minerals, compression, and then millions and millions of years. Also, I spent part of the summer reading *On the Origin of Species by Means of Natural Selection, or the Preservation of Favoured Races in the Struggle for Life* by Charles Darwin.

I see myself in a basement, shovelling shit out a window.

"What're you just standing there for?" I have discovered recently that he hates it when I look at him.

"You're a living fossil," I say.

He gets up, steps toward me.

"What the fuck did you just say?"

I drive the truck as fast as I can across the town to her house. People on the sidewalk stop and look at my truck. I stop pounding on her door when a man opens it. I recognize him from her stories.

"Can I help you?" he says.

I take a step back. My ears are stuffed with tiny violins. Trees bristle with the static of wings — birds on their way out.

"Is she here?"

"Is who here?"

I say her name.

"Yes, she's here. Can I tell her who's looking for her?"

He looks past my shoulder at the truck.

"Where do you live?" he says. "How do you know her?"

She slides up, beside his elbow. "What's going on?"

"Do you know this girl?" her father asks her.

He angles his logger's body towards hers. More than half the men in town are loggers and the other half work in the mill. On windy days, the mill blankets the town with a smell exactly like rotten eggs burning in an old cast-iron pan.

"No," she says. "I don't know her."

"Sorry," he says. "It seems you have the wrong house."


The next afternoon, she folds socks in the laundry room and pretends not to hear my fingernails, palms, then knuckles against the glass. She opens the window an inch.

"Are you crazy? The neighbours will hear."

"Let me in."

"I can't."

"Why not?" My clothes are filthy from sleeping in the truck last night.

"My father heard about the dance."

"Does he know about us?" She doesn't answer, holds her arm against the window so I can't open it any further. "What did you tell him?"

"He saw how you were looking at me. But he already knew."

"How?"

"Please leave. The neighbours will hear."

"How?"

"Last year. They wanted me to leave. He told them it wouldn't happen again."

"You told me I was the first."

"Was I yours?"

My knees are numb from kneeling and fear.

"Yes." I put my fingers through the small opening in the window. Her skin feels like stone. "Please let me in."

"I'll be cast out," she says.

I push the window the rest of the way open.

"Hell."

I climb onto the laundry machine and then jump down to the floor.

"Close the window," she says. "The neighbours will hear."

I close the window. It is as if all of the muscles in her body give up and stop when I touch her. She lets me lie her back on the pile of laundry to be washed. His laundry. All the smells of this place rise around our bodies. Wood shavings, sweat. I grasp fat handfuls of her skirt, her everyday uniform.

During those hours in the pit as we made love under the truck, she often raged against this skirt, against the husband her father has chosen. I saw him at the dance. He was the one who led her out of the cheering circle on the floor. He was lean and caramel-coloured, smooth as an adolescent deer. I am humiliated that he is the one who will have her. Her hands clench together behind my neck. There is a permanent bruise where her thumbs dig in. When that dark imprint fades, I will have lost her from my body.

I fall again and again into her and we are back in the turtle pit, protected by dark walls. I fall again and we sink farther, into the rock, and all the way down. Her hair lies across the floor like a vein of brilliant ore in the linoleum.

"I can't leave. This is my home," she says.

"What does that mean?"

She looks at me closely, as if she pities me.

"It means that this is where I'll stay until I die. It means that this is where I want to be buried."

It is raining when I climb onto the surface of the earth. I drag my legs out of the window behind me like thick, wet roots. A smear of white paint on dark glass — a face watches me through another basement window.

The sun makes the black pit an oven. I carry armfuls of rock to the middle of the pit and pull it apart. I sit and study the imprints inside, preserved there like an ancient form of plate photography. A pit of fossils is a good place to be desperate for messages. I stare at the insides of rocks until my eyes sting and run. A large chunk falls into two parts in my hands. Inside, a network of marks like light scratches on a blackboard, too small and faint to identify. Were they tiny worms, or the last traces of something bigger that wasn't preserved? I search for a pattern until I realize that they were still in motion when this happened to them. I open more rocks. A fern's tip, the torso of a prehistoric insect. Her curved neck, the hourglass of her body.

The truck coming sounds like an avalanche in the distance. I watch the four men come down the steep road. When I see what her father holds in his hand, I stand. I hold my fossils up like weapons.

The first blow brings blindness. The sky lunges upward and darkness crumbles off the world like a wall of rock. My body falls again and again. Every time I fall, I open my eyes and see the turtles, watching this. They tell me the story of when it happened to them — how the cloud of dust came and covered the earth in a day, put their bodies far under the layers of the earth. The enormous green ocean they swam through, the fish and creatures that were their world, patterns of leaves, patterns of tide, the banks where they mated under the moon that stayed safe from the fire. It happened without reason. There was no warning except for a change of temperature in the air. It happened to us and now it is happening to you, they tell me. What you are, we once were.

# LONG

# WAY

# FROM

# NOWHERE

"**SHIT**, we're a long way from nowhere," Derek said and black water came pouring down the mountain like a vein just got slit way down in all that rock.

"Long way from nowhere from what," I said.

"Quiet."

He rolled the window down and when his head came back into the truck it was wet and his face was red, slapped up by wind. His eyes shone blue and dark through his wet glasses. "Shit."

"What're we gonna do?" I said.

"Long way from fucking nowhere," he said again, just to himself.

No light. Trees stood across the top of the mountain above us like a line of men bigger than him, arms straight out, legs spread. Thunder. He started to count.

"One two three four."

Lightning cut the trees into black glass, silver shining between each of their needles. Screaming and blowing light.

"Oh oh oh."

"We gotta keep driving."

I looked down through the windshield and the road was gone. Where the road used to be there was a brown river slithering downward. All along the edges, roots went spidering under trees, holding them up. I'd never seen so many roots before. Rough brown of the forest on top, then white bone pushing into cracks in the rock of the mountain. Those roads were cut by the logging companies right into the sides of mountains and hills — wherever they needed to get to cut down the trees.

"Why're there so many roots?"

"Because it's a fucking wash-out. Whole road's washed right out."

"I'm cold."

"There's a blanket behind the seat. We're not wasting any of the battery on heat. Don't get it now. Hold on."

The road was a river and we were going down it.

Moving slower than the water coming down and down the mountain, spreading across the road so thin and fast it looked hard. Thunder again. This time he didn't count. Lightning made the world hard to look at and I put my head down, pushed my knees into my ears, blocking the sound out. The wheels cried and the truck drowned in watery noise as if we'd fallen into the ocean and storm waves were smashing into and into the thin metal doors. His hand landed heavy around the top of my head. I moved down under its weight, slipped down and curled up on the floor.

For a long time there was darkness.

Every few minutes, he honked the horn, but I thought the rain was so hard, no way anyone could hear us over the water.

"Hey there, you need any help?"

A man's voice. A truck door's flat slam. Morning sunlight shone off the worn-out vinyl seats, made them bright as polished stone. I hauled myself up onto my seat, stretched my body, sore from sleeping curled up on the floor.

"You got a kid in there?"

"Yeah, yeah, that's my girl," Derek said. "Jesus, storm made a mess of everything."

"What you doin all the way out here?"

Through the mud-lashed windshield I watched Derek glance back at me, send a silent warning. The stranger, dressed in a navy blue shirt and jeans and black boots, watched me closely over Derek's shoulder, his hand resting on his belt. I smiled obediently at a spot somewhere above the radio/gun.

"Oh you know. Just taking her for a drive for the day you know. Out in the bush. Gold-panning, swimming, shit like that. Kid stuff. Got stuck last night when the road washed out. Figured I should just stop, you know, wait it out, but then the truck got swamped."

Right away I hoped the guy with the angry voice didn't look inside the big rubber boxes chained down in the back of the truck. That's where we kept everything. Sleeping bags, pants and shirts and sweaters, plates and cups, bags of rice and cans of ravioli and whatever else I could put under my shirt in a store in the last town we went through.

"Where you from?"

"Just up from Campbell River," Derek said, giving the name of a town we'd passed through a few hours before the highway dwindled to a knotted brown rope and we faded into bush. "Can you give us a hand? Down pretty deep in this mud see."

"Yeah sure. I'll back my truck up. Your kid hungry?"

"She's tired, she's fine."

"No I'm not!"

Derek looked mad when I jumped out of the truck and ran up, but I knew it was my only chance to talk to the stranger, the first one in weeks. I waved my hand and introduced myself.

"I'm Banana."

"Hi Banana," he said. "I'm Mitchell."

"It's because of Shoshana," I said.

"This is my daughter Anna," Derek said. "This is, uh, Mitchell. He's gonna help us."

From the way Mitchell looked at me, I must have looked pretty bad from sleeping on the floor of the truck. I pressed my fingers to my cheek where the mat's pattern had pressed my skin. Hot, deep grooves like welts.

"It's because I slept on the floor," I said.

Derek put a hand on my shoulder.

"What happened to the road?"

"You just noticed?"

The road was twice as wide as I remembered it. Water rushing the ditches, dark runoff. The road was smooth as a floor, fine pale dirt washed over it, like the sun-thinned silt at low tide. Shreds of forest — trees cracked in half with their dark heads ploughing into the dirt, branches thrown around like someone had gone at everything laughing and swirling a chainsaw. "Some storm," Derek said.

"Yeah. Rain made swiss cheese of this part of the island. You should see what it's like farther north. Lots of road washed right out, this one did okay."

"Lot of guys out today?"

I could tell that Derek was nervous from the way he rolled his shoulders back one notch. When we saw a truck coming, we always took the next turn, sometimes sitting for hours in the dark cover of trees. That was how we'd lived since I could remember, driving around and around this part of the island where logging roads were thick as ant tunnels. There were so many, a person could spend their life driving around and around these invisible roads.

"Logging company's got some crews cleaning up a couple roads, only ones they're using though, you know," Mitchell said. "This one's pretty done. You're lucky I seen your truck up here from the main road or I wouldn't have come up here."

"Yeah, good thing."

"Tree huggers over there a way. They give you trouble, just go around em."

"Tree huggers?"

"Yeah. Haven't given me much trouble lately but just a heads-up, you know. I'll pull you out of that mud and take you down and around it, show you the way out."

"Appreciate it."

"Glad to."

They looked at each other the way I'd seen stray dogs look at each after all the sniffing was over. Mitchell took two granola bars out of the pocket of his jacket. The jacket was made of a shiny, stiff material, something expensive and safe.

He unwrapped both the bars, picked up my right hand, and closed my fingers around the bars, the granola feeling rough and warm, his thick fingers around my fingers, their undersides smooth as the bark of a sapling. "Have something to eat while we get your dad's truck outta that mud." I wanted him to let go of my hands.

"She's fine, we brought food," Derek said.

I sat on the side of a cedar while they hooked the two trucks together. They monitored each other through their windows while the mud that had half-buried the tires of our truck tried to suck it back down, drink it up completely. His wheels spun and he swore until finally Mitchell's truck — twice as tall as Derek's, its nose shaped like a spaceship — lunged. The mud made a hungry sucking sound, the mud disappointed to let the truck go.

"You coming or what?" Derek yelled and slapped the side of the truck. A sound that went up to the burned after-storm sky. I looked up. Birds were starting to re-emerge, circle.

As we started to drive, he said, "Push your hair out of your eyes and clean the dirt off your cheek. Right cheek. No, my right." Normally, he never said anything about how I looked. "Get your jacket from the back and put that on."

We followed Mitchell down the road off the small mountain, past the damage done by the storm. We thumped over small trees that had fallen across, like road bumps back in the city. The water charging down the creeks toward the ocean looked like my arm muscles twitching after swimming a long time. We passed a few clear-cuts that the water washed over, tilted lakes gleaming black in new sun.

"This guy's got his eye on you," Derek said, staring through the windshield as Mitchell glanced back at us again and again, waving, making sure we were staying with him. "Just stay quiet till we're on past wherever he stops."

"Who is he?" I said.

We knew who lived in the bush — students from Quebec who couldn't get the money to get home after the summer work was done and stayed through the rainy fall until the cold drove them back to a city or town; and backpackers who went around looking for the ghost towns and abandoned cabins; and guys from the logging company who drove huge trucks and always left their garbage at their camps and always drove down the middle of the road; and other part-time wanderers, benign outliers — birdwatchers, mushroom pickers, teenagers looking for the old mine pits to ride their motorbikes up and down their sides, and once in a while an adventurous, disappointed tourist.

Mitchell shaved and his truck looked expensive, something he couldn't have bought for himself. His jacket, its perfect folds and buttons encircled by red stitches.

"Must be from the government, from emergency relief or something, someone they sent up to look around if people got trapped in the storm," Derek said. Each time Mitchell waved, Derek smiled and so did I.

"Like we did."

"I would've got us out on my own. Got cardboard in the back. And a shovel."

"Nice of him to show us where to drive out."

"He's not leadin us out, Banana. He's makin sure we leave."

"Oh."

We sat side by side on the front seat, bouncing together, edging forward past destroyed forest and brush, the man's suspicious eyes pulling us forward, and Derek put his hand out across the gearshift under the line of the glass, under the other man's sightline, and took my hand.

I didn't know then, living with Derek in the bush, that I was homeless. Every day was full. Waking, washing in a river or lake or the surf of the icy Pacific if we were parked near a beach, fishing or finding berries and mushrooms and watching Derek struggle with the dented green propane stove with its propped-up lid and one coiled element that made it look like a broken-down record player. Derek never wanted to waste power on light so the end of the sun meant the end of our day. Sometimes I was wakened in the middle of the night by a quiet drive to a logging camp, the forest mumbling like a box full of affectionate people, where he would pull up beside one of their trucks, take the long rubber tube from the glove compartment, and jump silently out to siphon some gas. It was easy, he told me, except that you had to have the timing down — you had to know how to take a suck of air from the tube to get the suction going without getting a mouth full of gas. That hadn't happened to him for years. He had it all down to a rhythm now. I was frightened of the tube. I avoided opening the glove compartment because the tube would flop and leap out at me, a joke rubber snake or two arms of an elastic man flinging open to wrap around me and wrestle me still.

We followed Mitchell's truck along the torn edge of island for half an hour or so. In some places it was hard to tell where trees had been mowed down by logging or by the storm.

Derek reminded me every few minutes not to look upset when Mitchell stared back at us through his back window. I wondered if Mitchell knew how obvious these checks were, his face intent and large in the window. That proved he wasn't a cop, Derek said.

"What in holy hell," Derek said when the road filled up with naked bodies.

Mitchell stopped and started a few times, jolting forward, leaning into his horn, before he stopped for good, surrounded. "What the fuck is this," Derek said, brakes screaming.

Dancing, they were dancing. At first I'd thought they were fighting. They grabbed each other and flung their forms of pink and white around the dirt road. Three created a pyramid, a woman's feet wobbling on the shoulders of two spread-eagled men, her breasts swinging freely, her smile wide and directed not at us but upward at the trees and the arrowed span of the sky. Behind the pyramid, the tree people swarmed Mitchell's white government truck, scaled its wheels, flipped his side mirrors in and out like the protruding eyes of a giant cartoon insect. Mitchell sounded his horn over and over, then held his hand down on — a flat drone that emptied out the peace of the forest. I could see bodies lying across Mitchell's windshield. Flattened ass cheeks under glass. Their ecstatic mouths.

A man who looked like Jesus and moved his hips like a woman waved at me, his eyes clinging to mine. I slid downward, suddenly shy.

Mitchell gunned his engine and all the dancers went still and lay down on the road. They formed fleshy mounds around the wheels — the wheels looked like the dark seed centres of layered, pink flowers. I looked for the man who had smiled at me and saw his face framed by a knee and an elbow, smiling with a serenity I couldn't understand.

When Mitchell opened his door and swung his feet down, I expected hands to grab out at him, drag him downward, but instead the bodies shifted noiselessly, almost politely, to create a path, then instantly moved back into position.

Giggles chewed at his work boots as he walked.

"So those tree huggers I told you about?" Mitchell said.

"These're them?"

"Yep. We just got to wait it out for a bit," Mitchell said, as if the resting crowd of people were another storm, less severe than last night's.

"This is all of em?"

"Way more back at those tree houses of theirs. But yeah, this is all this is gonna be for now. They don't do this so often now. Mostly they keep to themselves. Probably they're doin this because you're here. Think they can get TV folks out here because you've got a kid."

"Tree houses?"

"Yeah. You don't know about that?"

"Tree houses?" I said and Mitchell stared at me. He took a

granola bar out of his pocket and tossed it to me. I wondered how many granola bars he had in his pocket and whether I could sneak over and steal some from his truck later while they talked.

"Been on TV quite a bit, surprised you never heard of it. This camp they've got way up in some really old trees."

"Oh, yeah, yeah, think I saw something like that a while back, yeah."

Mitchell raised his eyebrows and took the opportunity to scan the inside of our truck for the first time. The crumpled forestry maps that showed all the logging roads on this part of the island. An extra pair of boots, a broken satellite phone, an empty Cheerios box I'd smashed in with my shoulder sleeping on the floor last night, the Fanta bottle full of the seagull and eagle feathers I teased out of driftwood on beaches and was saving them until I had enough for a necklace. "Well just sit tight, okay then. That phone working?"

"Nope. Broke."

"You need to make a call? I got a phone in my truck."

Derek hesitated again. Sometimes I could hear his thoughts and predict his words, as if he were speaking through me. "Nice of you to offer, thanks. But we live on our own in town. Her mom died last year."

"Sorry to hear that."

I was accustomed to Derek's stories, had seen him work his way around countless people with his shape-shifting sentences. I looked sadly at my knees and remained still long enough for Mitchell to become uncomfortable and end the conversation by slapping the side of the truck, as if rewarding a good dog. An upbeat slap, a closing note. "Okay then. I'll radio in. Shouldn't be more than an hour, most."

We watched him call it in on his handheld.

"Wonder what the bastard's saying," Derek said. "Mitchell here. Yeah, still clean-shaven. Surrounded by sleeping naked people. Nope, no immediate threat. Once in a while a tit flops over real hard. Over." Derek eyed everything with tough suspicion. He expected the worst and hated to be disappointed. When I think of him now, I remember his chipped front tooth that made his occasional smile slightly menacing, the tooth's missing sharp edge like the contour of a white hook he kept hidden in his mouth.

"Why're all these people naked?" I said.

He sighed. His sighs and snores sounded the same — hard-blown sounds from the depth of his huge chest. "It's because of . . . a long time ago, in the nineteen sixties, there were lots of people who figured they didn't like what was going. It was mostly about war. The environment too. These people are kind of like those people. They're out there because some of the trees around here are very old."

"How old?"

"Hundreds of years old, some." He glared through the windshield at the road full of peaceful bodies. "Some've been here forever, I guess, I don't know," he added, and took Mitchell's granola bar from my hand and snapped it in half.

I watched them lying there, so still, and wondered how they could stay pressed to the damp of the earth, and how their skin could look so white, not dirty at all. I became dirty the second I put on clothes. They hung, as motionless and peaceful as sleeping fish drifting below the surface of the water in a large sunlit tank.

When the air around the trees purpled, Mitchell radioed in again.

Fifteen minutes later, four more white trucks roared up. Six men dressed like Mitchell jumped out, their matching eyes recording our presence. Hands and boots.

"Okay! Up up up up up!" they shouted.

The tree people didn't move. Instead, they looked more relaxed.

Shoulders and hips sank and settled."Up up up up!" the tree people chanted.

Large hands closed over shoulders and bodies were dragged up and hauled toward the roadside, dropped into bushes and onto the roots of the giant trees, tossed limply against trunks, their bodies falling heavy as bags of sand. None of the tree people fought back but I hid my eyes with my fingers, looked up when the screaming started.

Mitchell passed our windshield, one woman under each of his arms, and behind him two men from the trucks were holding cans and moving them back and forth, as if applying a layer of glossy paint.

"Oh shit. Pepper spray. Now they'll take our names for sure," Derek said and looked at me, the muscles around his eyes jumping.

The tree people rolled and wailed. Some got up and ran for the trees.

"Just stay calm," Derek said, putting a hand around my shoulder. "They're just taking care of things."

White bodies vanished into the forest as if plunging into a black curtain and their screaming faded quickly.

A few bodies remained on the road, polished with the layer of pale light that seemed to hang just over the floor of the forest.

Mitchell and the other men kicked at their shoulders. "Up up up up!" Their black boots larger than the white shoulders.

Once, when I was four or five, I'd seen a man beating a dog in an alley. The dog had curled in, taken the pain, cried and snarled into its belly, as if it wanted to eat itself alive, beginning with its guts.

The blast of cold air when I swung the door wide and jumped into the world.

"Stop!"

They raised their pepper spray cans again, let them drop and laughed when they saw who had spoken.

"What're you doing?" I said. "Stop it."

The four tree people at their toes rolled and groaned. A line of blood divided one cheek precisely, like the small hand on a clock.

"Banana! What the fuck are you doing? Banana!"

Derek's feet heavy behind me. Hand on my shoulder, pulling me back. Mitchell raised his hand, there was something in his hand. It was a radio/gun, it was something. I was in the dirt, dust forced my eyes and mouth shut. I crawled and ran. I looked up.

The tree people were all standing now, some doubled over, getting back the breath that had been kicked out of them. One of them was the man who had smiled at me earlier while his body had twisted freely across the road, feet scuffling and sweeping it clean, heels turning and polishing the dirt. Blood on his cheek. He put his hand out, a white line in the air. I stumbled forward and put my hand on his palm. It felt cold and smooth, like the skin of a plant, not hot and meaty like Derek's. I still don't know whether I went toward Yggdrasil or whether he pulled me forward.

Men stepped forward like weather closing in.

One of Yggradil's arms hooked under my elbow and I felt how little I weighed when he spun me up and I alighted on his back, my hands open on his chest, my fingers on his bare skin, the bones in his shoulders blunt and fine inside my elbows. I heard Derek and Mitchell bellowing, looked down at the grey line of the road's edge as we crossed it, and then I pressed my face into Yggdrasil's back to hide from the lashing strength of the branches, and I could see nothing around us. Just the feeling of his warm bare skin, a heat I wrapped myself around as the dark wet of the forest closed in around us.

Voices fell from the darkness of the sky. He shouted "Am I the last one?" and the voices called down yes, yes, Yggdrasil, that he was, and he muttered, my head wedged into the back of his neck, so that I was the only one who heard, "Oh thank God."

"Where are we?" I said as he put me down.

A woman landed on her feet in front of us. She stared at me. "You fucking brought a kid?" Two long rough cords of dark hair hung against her shoulders and her skin and teeth and eyes shone like waxpaper and bone.

"Let's go up and I'll tell you about it," Yggdrasil said.

"Shit, this is kidnapping."

"No, no."

The way he shook his head made me wonder what he knew. "Why not?"

"Come on, let's just go up."

"I'll have to tie her to you so you can climb."

"Okay."

"Are you hungry?" the woman said. "My name's Happy."

"Banana," I said.

"Hi Banana." She was the first adult who didn't question my chosen name.

"Where'd you come from?" I said.

She jabbed an index finger at the trunk of the tree behind her.

"Oh you're the people with the tree houses," I said, remembering what Mitchell had said.

"Did you see us on TV?" Happy said.

"No. That guy, Mitchell, he said it to Derek."

"Who's Derek?"

"My friend who I travel with."

Happy's face turned but she just nodded and Yggdrasil said, "Let's go up. I'm starving. You know how long we were lying on that road?"

They couldn't put down ladders, they told me later, because the ladders would be smashed up by the wind or the RCMP. They used heavy ropes and clamps. They could climb up and down like monkeys, hips and shoulders skimming the coarse bark of the camp's central tree, Raven. Happy tied me to Yggdrasil's back and he told me, "Don't hang on tight, it'll just make you even heavier."

Halfway up the two-hundred-foot tree, Yggdrasil paused for breath and I pulled my face from his neck and forced myself to look at where we were.

The ground we'd flown over was invisible now, a depthlessness. Looking straight out, trunks of trees sliced up the air, each empty space a slightly different shade of green, the shadows of branches sweeping softly back and forth. Up there I could see that trees weren't still but constantly swaying, making small circles in the air, huge solemn dancers, their motion impossible to see from their roots. I hadn't expected the amount of sound, a steady rushing of wind.

I looked up and saw a network, a spidering of paths reaching off into the darkness.

Months earlier, Derek and I had driven past a clutch of men and women camped at the side of a logging road, playing drums and wearing brightly striped sweaters, a long board painted with the words IF A TREE FALLS IN THIS FOREST grasped by what seemed like dozens of hands.

"Fucking hippies," Derek had said, after reading the sign aloud to me. "Why can't they just get jobs like everybody else?" I'd wondered, briefly, how Derek could ask that, since he didn't have a job, got by on scrounging forest food and siphoning gas from forestry trucks and sending me into places to steal. I had an innocent face, he told me. He taught me how my face and smile could be a toy power.

But he had a truck, I told myself, so it was different. Once in a while we drove to a town halfway down the island and he picked up an envelope from a P.O. box in a 7-Eleven, came back to the truck with a coconut chocolate bar, a litre of Pepsi, and a copy of every newspaper. I asked him to read the newspapers aloud to me, but he never did.

"She met Mitchell," Happy said, and the circle of tree people looked at me intensely.

They'd come crawling and tumbling into Yggdrasil's tree house soon after we'd arrived. The three others who'd stayed on the road with Yggdrasil were recognizable from their bruises.

Happy had cleaned the blood from Yggdrasil's cheek with her sleeve.

"You know Mitchell?" a woman asked. I'd never seen a bald woman before.

"No," I said, shoving bread and apple slices and chunks of bitter waxy chocolate into my mouth from the cracked plate Happy passed around the circle. "No, he just came and found us and pulled Derek's truck out of the mud. He wanted us to leave, or that's what Derek said. We got stuck in the storm."

A man asked, "Is she safe?" No one seemed to hear him. A heavy white stone hung from his neck. He hadn't been on the road.

"We lost one house in the storm," Yggdrasil said. "No one was in it when it went down."

The inside walls of Yggdrasil's house were made of plywood, cardboard, squares of thin metal hammered together with tiny bent nails. A heap of pillows and blankets in one corner, a plastic crate full of food, a metal drum with a pipe sticking out of it that went through a small hole in the wall. One wall of the tree house was the curved trunk of the camp's central tree. Cut off from the rest of the tree, the section of bark looked like cliff-face.

I watched Yggdrasil light the wide cardboard wick of a sludge of wax in a tin can, place a tin can full of coal over that, and a small pot of water over that.

"Who's Mitchell?" I said.

That was when I knew that Yggdrasil was the leader; all the tree people waited for him to answer.

"Mitchell has a job with the government," he began slowly. "He's paid to care about things that are different than the things we care about."

"Like what?"

"Some people think that it's good to get a lot of money from cutting these trees down." He looked at me quietly. Derek had taught me how to use silence to make people uncomfortable — to force them to do something. *Just stay quiet,* he'd told me, *and wait for the other person to make the next move.* I looked at my hands and waited for Yggdrasil to do something. When I looked back up at him I realized that he knew what I knew, that he could see what I was doing, and panic paced its itch over my back.

"Why?" I said.

"This tree was fifty feet tall when Columbus landed in America. And people like Mitchell think it should be cut down to make toilet paper." His voice smoothed to a point.

"I love using toilet paper," I said and wondered why all the tree people began to laugh, some of them bending over, cross-legged. Two of them were Chinese, a few of the women had muscled arms and cropped hair, one man was missing a front tooth, and one woman was wearing her hair wrapped around her head like a shining gold bandana.

"Everybody, this is Banana," Yggdrasil said.

"Hi Banana."

They introduced themselves. Some of their names were normal — Greg, Andy, Lauren, Jed. Then there was Sedna, Red Bear and Rootlove. There was Star and Sky and Welcome and Chuckle.

"I'm Yggdrasil."

"What?"

"It means," Happy leaned over to tell me, "the Norse tree of life."

"What?"

"Welcome," Yggdrasil said. "You are free to leave whenever you like. The trees are here for everyone."

When he said that, I thought that he was probably crazy. I remembered something about an island where people with the same horrible disease were sent. I wondered if this was like that place, why anyone would live in a tree instead of on the ground with everybody else. Was it too late? Had I already caught their disease? So when Happy settled a hand on my shoulder and asked whether I'd like to sleep in her house in the next tree — she would carry me across the walkway — I pulled my body away violently.

The man with the white stone around his neck said, "Let's leave her alone now, we're frightening her." They rose one by one and quietly left. In the darkness, through the openings in Yggdrasil's walls, the walkways were invisible, and they looked like a flock of ghosts drifting off toward the roof of the forest.

The moon was a spotlight for the canopy, something you could reach out to turn on and off. Something close.

Yggradrasil took the boiling water off the can of coal and poured it into metal camping mugs, stirred in powder.

"How long have you been living up here?" I said.

"Almost a year," Yggdrasil said.

The roof of his tiny house was a tarp and as it started to rain the quiet drumming filled the space, thousands of tapping fingers massaging my brain and eyes.

"How high up are we?"

"About two hundred feet."

"That's really high."

"After a while you just forget about looking down."

Once, Derek had decided that the police were onto us. We'd passed too many trucks on the roads in the past few days. They were onto us. He repeated this, his eyes keeping the road from flipping up from the ground like tape. Worms of light squirmed in the dust of the ditches.

He drove to a beach and grabbed my hand and led me across, the hot sharp stones biting through the hole in the sole of my right shoe. My stomach roared and Derek told me he'd leave me with food. "Leave me?" I screamed and he pulled me harder.

Stacked ochre rocks at the end of the beach, tall as a building, and he pushed me ahead of him to the top. Behind the rocks, the cliffs, black, worked over with curtains of dangling roots, and in front of us, the ocean stretching endless.

The water wouldn't get into the cave when the tide rose, he told me. I'd be safe there because the cave was deeper than the waterline, but the entrance to the cave was right above that limit, a permanent stain of algae, life growing right into the rock.

The cave was a slick burrow and he lowered me into it, dropped his jacket and his backpack in after me. I hear the crackle of plastic packages in the backpack, remembered the chips he'd bought at a gas station a few days before. His voice weaved in and turned its form around me. "You'll be safe here. I'll come back for you tomorrow." I heard him waiting and listened to his high rabbit breaths. Wind blew over the mouth of the cave like breath over the mouth of a flute.

The ocean swelled and gathered around me, I felt its body like a sound. I was a thing hung inside an organ deep inside a huge, hungry animal. The waves rolled rhythm waterfisted and the light at the entrance of the cave dimmed, the air cooled, the tide rose and drunk the light down. When the part of sky I could see was finally black, I wondered if Derek had lied, if this was how he would get rid of me. Once the tide must have reached the mouth of the cave, maybe centuries before, because as I curled up on my side the stone was smooth, the clammy calm of a hidden person pressed against my cheek, soothing me.

As soon as the media found out that the protestors had taken someone's kid up to the tree village, all hell broke loose. The tree people hauled up the ropes and took shifts wearing earplugs so they could get some sleep against the country music the forest services vans blasted through PAs all day and night to drive them down from the trees.

RCMP pepper sprayed supporters from a nearby town who arrived with provisions to send up on ropes that were momentarily flung down. An army of TV journalists and RCMP circled the wagons, beat paths through the forest from the nearest road, shouted threats through a loudspeaker, put up signs beckoning me down: ANNA, YOUR FATHER MISSES YOU. Helicopters buzzed the tree houses. Tarps and tin and cardboard and lightweight wood shivered, hovered on the branches like huge stunned birds. Hours after the helicopters left, my ears rang, my head light as if I hadn't eaten in days. My bones hurt with the noise of sirens and loud speakers and engines and metal butchering air. Yggdrasil wrote messages on the silvery backs of pieces of bark and tied them to stones that he dropped toward the cameras and RCMP, a flickering black ocean of lenses and polished hats. He read them to me.

I couldn't read, but Happy told me calmly that she would teach me if I chose to stay in the village long enough. "We are here to speak for the trees," Yggdrasil read aloud to me. I tried to imagine the men with flashing arm bands reading these messages, their responding anger. "We are not keeping her here by force. She is free to leave when she wishes and we will assist her in leaving when she chooses. As we have said since the beginning, we will not come down to the ground until these trees are safe." After I approved each message, he dropped it, his hand flipping open with the strength and agility of a small animal. "We refuse to meet violence with violence," he read aloud to me.

He answered my questions with long, detailed stories — about the time the RCMP had burned down their base camp on the roots of the tree they called Raven; about the time they'd broken the ribs of a protestor lying down in front of a logging truck and had him sent to a hospital on the mainland where he couldn't be contacted by the tree people. The lightning storm when the tree people had stood on the branches, watching trees in the next valley go off like roman candles.

He told me that people only thought the tree people were crazy because they didn't know how much of the island had been logged. You could only see that from the air, from a helicopter or small low-flying plane. The vast clear-cuts the colour of sand and garbage. Tree planting, he said, had good intentions, but it wasn't the same as what he was doing. He wasn't going to waste time pouring cups of water into the ocean.

I told him my favourite foods and he dropped a piece of bark reading: "Dear RCMP and Derek: If you want to help Banana she

requests that you please send Cheerios, chocolate chip cook-
ies, mandarin oranges, gum, and shampoo. Peace, Yggdrasil."

The package arrived with a message from Derek tucked
into it:

*Hi Banana,*
*I'm very worried and I'm not mad at all! The RCMP have told me*
*that the protestors are not dangerous but they are breaking the law.*
*Please come down soon. Miss you. Dad*

I could tell that the note had been supervised by the RCMP, or
he wouldn't have signed it Dad.

Happy read the note. "Do you miss him?"

I shook my head.

There were a bunch of us sitting around in Yggdrasil's house,
eating handfuls of Cheerios Happy had brought from her house,
anchored to the tree named Blend.

Yggdrasil said, "I'll take you down now if you want."

"I can't go back," I said.

"Is he your father?" Yggdrasil said.

He was the only one who could have asked. They all seemed
relieved when he did. When I began to weep, slowly, a swarm
of fish being born in my belly, Happy moved a hand in a wide
circle on my back and repeated, "Settle, settle, settle, settle."

Yggdrasil could see through people, read their maps of hesitation and need and find where they were steady and touch
only those places at first, then move slowly to the others, like
a swimmer testing colder waters.

Dozens of hands covered my back, my shoulders, my arms,
then my hair. I rocked and wept and the wind made deep sound,

dark sound in the branches the thickness of bodies, as if the ancient tree to which we were anchored was the throat of the sky.

"The trees love you," Yggdrasil said and I laughed at him, then felt the laughs morph into the smaller shapes of sobs.

Over the two years I lived in the tree village, this is what Yggdrasil said instead of "I love you." Now, I wonder if he believed in human love at all.

I'd been living with the tree people for five or six days, though it felt like weeks. Days were marked by only the light that faded and arrived suddenly in the canopy. The tree people spent their time reading, talking, resting, and listening to a radio operated with a large crank on its side. The radio recited news of my abduction by the protestors, how they'd confined me to one of the houses and refused to accept provisions, how I was being used as a hostage, leverage for the contract they wanted signed by the two logging companies, the RCMP, and forest services. After the second day, Derek's voice, reciting pleas for my release, stopped, and only the reporters continued. News of the eco-terrorists, the anarchists in the trees, the blood feud between the hippies and the loggers. When they gave up their camp, the leaders would be charged with a long list of crimes.

I'd spent the last few days wandering among the houses. The white-haired man had cornered me and asked aggressively if I was Mitchell's spy. He rarely left his house, rang a brass bell when it was time to sit and watch branches wander over each other, overlapping and pausing.

The RCMP sent up a note informing Yggrasil and Happy that there would be a raid the following afternoon unless I was returned. Social services had been unable to find Derek in their system and I was now a ward of the state.

During the night, Yggdrasil tied me to his back and we swung on a rope to a smaller tree outside the village. We scaled down the tree and crawled for an hour to a road. A woman with a bicycle was there waiting for us. I didn't ask how she got there; Yggdrasil's world was made of a web of fibrous connections that couldn't be asked about. She took me on her bicycle to a cabin several hours away and kept me there for a week. When she returned me to the village, the trucks and cameras were gone and the tree people had nearly finished rebuilding what had been destroyed by the raid. When I asked the old man wearing the white stone what had happened, he looked through me and said, not knowing that I knew the truth, "Pretty rough storm a few nights ago. Surprised you didn't hear it. Guess you slept right through."

A week later I was awakened by screams. I struggled out of the wool blanket Happy had folded for me on the floor of her house and staggered for the curtain that hung over the walkway that led to Yggdrasil's.

All of the tree people were crowded on the surrounding walkways, some on their hands and knees, staring downward. Yggdrasil stared downward, silent, his arms straight at his sides. He saw me and put a hand out. "Stay in there," he said.

A truck had been driven to the base of Raven and a small team of men was at work on the base of a nearby tree. The tree's house had been destroyed in the storm and scraps still clung to the branches. The throaty roar of a chainsaw starting up, then a second chainsaw, and then fine pitch of wood turning to powder. I saw Happy's arms twisting around her face like vines. Yggdrasil hurried me back into Happy's house and snapped the T-shirt curtain closed behind him.

"Are they doing that because of me?" I said.

"They don't know where you are. Don't go outside. Not for a while."

The sound of the chainsaws singing together, clashing with the shouts of the tree people. Two hundred feet up, the chainsaws sounded as if they were slicing into the tree beside my ear.

I hung back so I wouldn't be seen. Looking down, I saw the men, small as toys, crowded around the base of the tree they were cutting. Would they continue to cut trees for as long as I stayed? The clutch of seven trees to which the village was anchored was the oldest on the island, Yggdrasil had told me. If they were cut down and the logging company took all control of the area, no tree would ever grow here again to be this old.

Down on the ground, the men with the chainsaws. I looked harder and recognized one as Mitchell. I wondered what he knew about me. I wondered what Derek had told them. Not the truth. But I wondered what story he had made up about me, where I came from. Who I was, since I wasn't his daughter. Where had he found me? Sleeping on the steps of a church. Drifted to shore on a piece of shipwreck. Abandoned on a barstool in some dive. I raised a hand and waved at them and they continued to shout, their words torn from their mouths by the branches that reached out like hands to protect me. If I let go of the rope, I would fall two hundred feet and no one would ever know where I'd come from before Derek. Yggdrasil watched me from the doorway and the other tree people on the walkway didn't come near me as I stared down at the men, my hands gripping the rope railing hard. None of them said anything. What had Derek told them? I didn't want to know. It didn't matter what story he'd told them. I could have been the result of any story.

I looked down at the smallness of the men, my body floating on a dim green ocean. I held on to the rope and let it guide me back to Yggdrasil. I passed him and knelt on the floor of Happy's house and threw up until the sides of my neck ached with pulling, until the last hot strand had been unglued from the bottom of my stomach. My body a dry curled muscle.

It took them the rest of the afternoon and part of the evening to finish cutting the tree. It fell through the forest evening, a rope of shadow cutting a dark arc in the half-light, the sound of it crashing into underbrush like the sound of wave on rock. Over the next few hours we heard cracking and snapping as the tree settled in, like the sound of a body hauling itself over ice with metal wings.

Happy told me, running her fingers through my hair before bed, that tomorrow they would cut it up and take it to the mill to be cut into planks, the bark and outside round parts discarded or pulped. The next morning they didn't come back. The huge tree was left, lying on the floor of the forest.

They left it as an example, Happy said softly. Yggdrasil said, no, as a threat.

I watched him swing effortlessly down the rope and walk up and down the fallen tree that lay wide and straight as a road through the forest.

Vertical green world. We watched the emptiness close in around us, the clear-cuts join sides and become a landscape of dust. Often when I crept to the edge of the platform and looked down, I saw the outline of Derek, again and again, and then I saw him less. When they finally gave up their village, Yggdrasil and Happy were charged with my abduction. Ron and Sara Butler. They were siblings; I'd always assumed they were lovers.

The RCMP demanded: Who was I and where had I come from?

I remembered the night they'd rescued me. The woman on her dark bicycle. Percussion of leaves, breath, chains slipping in the brush. Leaving Derek behind on the forest floor.

"Nowhere," I told everyone.

Now I live on the ground.

## ACKNOWLEDGMENTS

Thank you to Lorraine Weir for her endless, generous support of this book; for being the first reader of these stories; darkness and light.

Jesse Marchand, loyal and cherished friend.

Joshie, Lucy and Adrian, canine co-authors.

Meredith Quartermain for generously organizing her group of Vancouver women writers at Rhizome, giving conversation and context over several years.

Linda Svendsen and Maureen Medved for early feedback on stories.

My sisters, Simone and Sabrina, and my parents.

The BC Arts Council for financial support.

Many of these stories first appeared in Canadian literary journals and anthologies, giving space and support that encouraged me to continue to write and publish. Thank you to *Prairie Fire* (ed. Andris Taskans), *Descant*, *The Fiddlehead* (ed. Mark Anthony Jarman), *Event* (ed. Rick Maddocks), *Joyland*, *09: Best Canadian Stories* (ed. John Metcalf, Oberon Press), *Coming Attractions 09* (ed. Mark Anthony Jarman, Oberon Press), and *Matrix* (ed. Jon Paul Fiorentino).

**ALEX LESLIE** is from Vancouver. Her chapbook of micro-fictions *Twenty Objects For The New World* was published by Nomados Press in 2011. Leslie's writing has been published in literary journals across Canada and in the *Best Canadian Stories* anthology series (Oberon Press). She has won a Gold National Magazine Award for personal journalism and a CBC Literary Award for fiction.